**"Emma."** Dante's gri[...] hands. **"What are y[...] [...] bad guy or me?"**

She blurted out, "I'm not afraid of either." Her head dipped and she stared at her boots. "I'm afraid of me."

His heart melted at the way her bottom lip wobbled. "Why?"

Her glance shifted to the corner of the room and she didn't say anything for a full ten seconds. "I've been independent for so long, I'm afraid of becoming dependent on anyone."

"Relying on someone else doesn't have to be a bad thing. And it's only temporary, then you can go back to being independent."

She didn't throw it back in his face, so he figured she was wavering. He went in for the clincher.

"Besides, you saved my life twice." He lifted one of her hands to his lips and pressed a kiss there. "I owe you."

# CHRISTMAS AT THUNDER HORSE RANCH

## Elle James

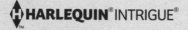

Recycling programs
for this product may
not exist in your area.

This book is dedicated to my fans who kept
writing, asking when Dante would have his
book. Without my fans I wouldn't be pursuing
the career I love. Thank you for reading and
falling in love with my characters.
May all your lives be blessed!

ISBN-13: 978-0-373-69792-2

CHRISTMAS AT THUNDER HORSE RANCH

Copyright © 2014 by Mary Jernigan

Printed in U.S.A.

HARLEQUIN®
www.Harlequin.com

## ABOUT THE AUTHOR

A Golden Heart Award winner for Best Paranormal Romance in 2004, Elle James started writing when her sister issued a Y2K challenge to write a romance novel. She has managed a full-time job and raised three wonderful children, and she and her husband even tried their hands at ranching exotic birds (ostriches, emus and rheas) in the Texas Hill Country. Ask her, and she'll tell you what it's like to go toe-to-toe with an angry 350-pound bird! After leaving her successful career in information technology management, Elle is now pursuing her writing full-time. Elle loves to hear from fans. You can contact her at ellejames@earthlink.net or visit her website at www.ellejames.com.

## Books by Elle James

HARLEQUIN INTRIGUE

*Covert Cowboys, Inc.

# CAST OF CHARACTERS

*Dante Thunder Horse*—Lakota Indian, former U.S. Army helicopter pilot, now working for the U.S. Customs and Border Protection, stationed at Grand Forks, North Dakota.

*Emma Jennings*—Shy, socially awkward professor of paleontology at the University of North Dakota in Grand Forks.

*Sheriff William Yost*—The sheriff the Thunder Horse men despise for the slipshod investigation of their father's death and who is now dating their mother.

*Ryan Yost*—The sheriff's son, raised by his Lakota mother on the reservation, who now owns a company that installs home and business security systems all over North Dakota.

*Monty Langley and Theron Price*—Oil speculators buying up mineral rights and land from local ranchers in the Badlands as oil production grows into a big business in North Dakota.

*Maddox Thunder Horse*—Oldest of the Thunder Horse brothers and a North Dakota rancher, who also cares for the wild horses of the Badlands.

*Katya Ivanov Thunder Horse*—Maddox's wife and a princess of a former Soviet Union country.

*Tuck Thunder Horse*—Dante's brother, member of the FBI, working out of the Bismarck regional branch.

*Julia Thunder Horse*—Tuck's wife and schoolteacher who lives with Tuck and their little girl, Lily, in Bismarck.

*Pierce Thunder Horse*—Dante's older brother, the one who left North Dakota to pursue a career in the FBI and is back working out of the Bismarck regional branch office alongside his brother Tuck.

*Rosalyn Thunder Horse*—Pierce's new wife and the owner of the Carmichael Ranch bordering the Thunder Horse Ranch in the Badlands of North Dakota, dividing her time between ranching and living with Pierce in Bismarck, where he works.

*Amelia Thunder Horse*—Mother to the Thunder Horse men, who lost her husband to a freak riding accident.

# Chapter One

Big sky...check. Flat plains...check. Storm clouds rolling in...check.

Like ticking off his preflight checklist, Dante Thunder Horse reviewed what was in front of him, a typical early winter day in North Dakota before the first real snowstorm of the season. It had been a strange December. Usually it snowed by Thanksgiving and the snow remained until well into April.

This year, the snow had come by Halloween and melted and still the ground hadn't yet grown solid with permafrost.

Based on the low temperature and the clouds rolling in, that first real snow was about to hit their area. The kids of Grand Forks would be excited. With the holidays just around the corner, they'd have their white Christmas after all.

A hundred miles away from base, flying the U.S.-Canadian border as an air interdiction agent, or pilot, for the Customs and Border Protection, Dante was on a mission to check out a possible illegal border crossing called in by a concerned citizen. A farmer had seen a man on a snowmobile coming across the Canadian border.

He figured it was someone out joyriding who didn't realize he'd done anything wrong. Still, Dante had to check.

He didn't expect anything wild or dangerously crazy to happen. The Canadian border didn't have near the illegal crossings as the southern borders of the United States. Most of his sorties were spent enjoying the scenery and observing the occasional elk, moose or bear sighting.

Chris Biacowski, scheduled to fly copilot this sortie, had come down with the flu and called in sick.

Dante was okay with flying solo. He usually liked having the quiet time. Unless he started thinking about his past and what his future might have been had things worked out differently.

Three years prior, he'd been fighting Taliban in Afghanistan. He'd been engaged to Captain Samantha Olson, a personnel officer who'd been deployed at Bagram Airfield. Every chance he got he flew over to see her. They'd been planning their wedding and talking about what they'd put on their dream sheet for their next assignments.

After flying a particularly dangerous mission where his door gunner had taken a hit, Dante came back to base shaken and worried about his crew member. He stayed with the gunner until he was out of surgery. The gunner had survived.

But Dante's life would be forever changed. When he had left on his mission, his fiancée had decided to go with a few others to visit a local orphanage.

On the way back, her vehicle hit an improvised explosive device. Three of the four people on board the military vehicle had died instantly. Samantha had survived long enough to get a call through to the base. By the time medics arrived, she'd lost too much blood.

Dante had constructed images in his mind of Samantha lying on the ground, the uniform she'd been so proud to wear torn, a pool of her own blood soaking into the desert sand.

He'd thought through the chain of events over and over, wondering if he'd gone straight from his mission to Bagram, would Samantha have stayed inside the wire instead of venturing out? Had their talk about the babies they wanted spurred her to visit the children no one wanted? Those whose parents had been collateral damage or killed by the Taliban as warning or retribution?

Today was the third anniversary of her death. When Chris had called in sick, Dante couldn't cancel the flight, and he sure as hell couldn't stay at home with his memories haunting him.

For three years, he'd pored over the events of that day, wishing he could go back and change things so that Samantha was still there. How was he expected to get on with his life when her memory haunted him?

The only place he felt any peace whatsoever was soaring above the earth. Sometimes he felt closer to Samantha, as if he was skimming the underbelly of heaven.

As he neared the general area of the farm in the report, movement brought his mind back to earth. A dark shape exploded out of a copse of trees, moving swiftly into the open. It appeared to be a man on a snowmobile. The vehicle came to a halt in the middle of a wide-open field and the man dismounted.

Dante dropped lower and circled, trying to figure out what he was up to. About the time he keyed his mic to radio back to headquarters, he saw the man unstrap what appeared to be a long pipe from the back of his snowmobile and fit something into one end of it.

Recognition hit, and Dante's blood ran cold. He jerked the aircraft up as quickly as he could. But he was too late.

The man on the ground fired a rocket-propelled grenade.

Dante dodged left, but the grenade hit the tail and exploded. The helicopter lurched and shuddered. He tried to keep it steady, but the craft went into a rapid spin. Realizing his tail rudder had probably been destroyed, Dante had to land and if he didn't land level, the blades could hit first, break off and maybe even end his life.

The chopper spun, the centrifugal force making it difficult for Dante to think and move. He reached up and switched the engines off, but not soon enough. The aircraft plummeted to the ground, a blade hit first, broke off and slammed into the next blade. The skids slammed against the ground and Dante was thrown against the straps of his harness. He flung an arm over his face as fragments of the blades acted like flying shrapnel, piercing the chopper's body and windows. The helicopter rolled onto its side and stopped.

Suspended by his harness, Dante tried to key the mic on his radio to report his aircraft down. The usual static was absent, the aircraft lying as silent as death.

Dante dragged his headset off his head. Frigid wind blew through the shattered windows and the scent of fuel stung his nostrils.

The sound of an engine revving caught Dante's attention. The engine noise grew closer, moving toward his downed aircraft. Had the predator come to finish off his prey?

He scrambled for the harness releases, finally finding and pulling on the quick-release buckles. He dropped on his left side, pain knifing through his arm. Gritting his teeth, he scrambled to his knees on the door beneath him and attempted to reach up to push against the passenger door. Burning pain stabbed his left arm again and he dropped the arm and worked with his good arm to fling the passenger-side door open. It bounced on its hinges and smashed closed again, nearly crushing his fingers with the force.

He hunched his shoulder and nudged the door with it, pushing it open with a little less force. This time, the door remained open and he stood, his head rising above the body of the craft. As he took stock of the situation, a bullet pinged against the craft's fuselage.

Dante ducked. A snowmobile had come to a stop a hundred yards away, the rider bent over the handlebars, pointing a high-powered rifle in his direction. With nothing but the body of the helicopter between him and the bullets, Dante was a sitting duck.

He sniffed the acrid scent of aviation fuel growing more potent as the time passed and more bullets riddled the exterior of the craft. If he stayed inside the helicopter, he stood a chance of the craft bursting into flames and being burned alive. If the bullets sparked a fire, the fuel would burn. If the flames reached the tanks, it would create a tremendous explosion.

Out of the corner of his eye, he could see the bright orange flicker of a flame. In seconds, the ground surrounding his helicopter was a wall of fire.

Amid the roar of flames, the snowmobile revved and swooped closer.

Debating how long he should wait before throwing himself out on the ground, Dante could feel the heat of the flames against his cheeks. If he didn't leave soon, there wouldn't be anything left for the attacker to shoot.

The engine noise faded, drowned out by the roar of the fire.

With fire burning all around him, Dante pulled himself out of the fuselage one-armed and dropped to the ground. His shoulder hit a puddle of the flaming fuel and his jumpsuit ignited.

Rolling through the wall of flames, Dante couldn't get the flame to die out. His skin heated, the fuel was thoroughly soaked into the fabric. He rolled away from the flame, onto his back, unzipped the flight suit and shimmied out of it before the burning fabric melted and stuck to his skin.

Another bullet thunked into the earth beside Dante. Wearing nothing but thermal underwear, Dante rolled over in the snow, hugging the ground, giving his attacker very little target to aim at.

Covered in snow, with nothing to defend himself, Dante awaited his fate.

EMMA JENNINGS HAD spent the morning bundled in her thermal underwear, snow pants, winter jacket, earmuffs and gloves, one of them fingerless. Yes, it was getting colder by the minute. Yes, she should have given up two days ago, but she felt like she was so close, and the longer she waited, the harder the ground got as permafrost transformed it from soft dirt to hard concrete.

The dig had been abandoned by everyone else months ago when school had started up again at the University of North Dakota. Emma came out on weekends hoping to get a little farther along. Fall had been unseasonably warm with only one snowfall in late October that had melted immediately. Six inches of snow had fallen three days ago and seemed in no hurry to melt, though the ground hadn't hardened yet. The next snowfall expected for that evening would be the clincher, with the predicted two feet of snow.

If she hadn't set up a tent around the dig site months ago, she never would have come. As it was, school was out and she'd come with her tiny trailer in tow, with the excuse that she needed to pull down the tent and stow it for the winter. If not for the steep roof, the tent would easily collapse under the twenty-four inches of white powder. Not to mention the relentless winds across the prairie would destroy the tent if it was left standing throughout the wicked North Dakota winter.

Each weekend since fall semester began had proved to be fair and Emma had gone out to dig until this weekend. Some had doubted there'd be snow for Christmas. Not Emma. She'd lived in North Dakota all her life, and never once in her twenty-six years had the snow missed North Dakota at Christmas.

So far, the dig had produced the lower jawbone of a *Tyrannosaurus rex.* Emma was certain if she kept digging, she'd find the skull of the animal nearby. The team of paleontologists and students who'd been on the dig all summer had unearthed neck bones, and near the end of the summer, the jawbone. The skull had to be close. She just needed a little more time.

There to tear down the tent before it was buried in knee-deep drifts, she'd ducked inside to find the ground smooth and dry and the dirt just as she'd left it the weekend before. She squatted to scratch away at the surface with a tool she'd left behind. Before she knew it, she'd succumbed to the lure of the dig. That had been two days ago.

Knowing she had to leave before the storm hit, she'd given herself half of the last day to dig. Immersed in her work, the sound of a helicopter cut through her intense concentration and she glanced at her watch. With a gasp, she realized just how long she'd been there and that it was nearing sunset of her last day on the site.

She still needed to get the tent down and stowed before

dark. With a regretful glance at the ground, she pushed the flap back and ducked through. High clouds blocked out any chance for warmth or glare from the sun.

The thumping sound of blades churning the air drew her attention and she glanced at the sky. About a mile away, a green-and-white helicopter hovered low over the prairie.

From where she stood, she couldn't see what it was hovering over. The ground had a gentle rise and dip, making the chopper appear to be almost on the ground. Emma recognized the craft as one belonging to the Customs and Border Protection.

There was a unit based out of Grand Forks and she knew one of the pilots, Dante Thunder Horse, from when he'd taken classes at the university. A handsome Native American, he had caught her attention crossing campus, his long strides eating up the distance.

He'd taken one of her anthropology classes and they'd met in the student commons on a couple of occasions and discussed the university hockey team games. When he'd finally asked her out, she'd screwed up enough courage to take him up on it, suggesting a coffee shop where they'd talked and seemed to hit it off.

Then nothing. He hadn't called or asked her out for another date. He must have finished his coursework at the university because she hadn't run into him again. Nor did she see him crossing campus. She'd been disappointed when he hadn't called, but that was at the end of last spring. The summer had kept her so busy on the dig, she wouldn't have had time for a relationship—not that she was any good at it anyway. Her longest one had lasted two months before her shyness had scared off the poor young man.

Emma wondered if Dante was the pilot flying today.

She marveled at how close the helicopter was. In all the vastness of the state, how likely was it that the aircraft would be hovering so near to the dig? Then again, the site was fairly close to the border and the CBP was tasked with protecting the northern border of the United States.

As Emma started to turn back to her tent to begin the job of tearing it down, a loud bang shook the air. Startled, she saw a flash in her peripheral vision from the direction of the helicopter. When she spun to see what had happened, the chopper was turning and turning. As if it was a top being spun faster and faster, it dropped lower and lower until it disappeared below the rise and a loud crunching sound ripped the air.

Her heart stopped for a second and then galloped against her ribs. The helicopter had crashed. As far away from civilization as they were, there wasn't a backup chopper that could get to the pilot faster than she could.

Abandoning her tent, she ran for the back of the trailer, flung open the utility door in the rear, dropped the ramp and climbed inside. She'd loaded the snowmobile on the off chance she couldn't get the truck all the way down the road to the dig. Fortunately, she'd been able to drive almost all the way to the site and had parked the truck and trailer on a hardstand of gravel the wind had blown free of snow near the edge of the eight-foot-deep dig site.

Praying the engine would start, she turned the key and pressed the start button. The rumble of the engine echoed off the inside of the trailer but then it died. The second time she hit the start button, the vehicle roared to life. Shifting to Reverse, she backed down the ramp and turned to face the direction the helicopter had crashed.

A tower of flames shot toward the sky, smoke rising in a plume.

Her pulse pounding, Emma raced across the snow, headed for the fire.

As she topped the rise, her heart fell to her knees. The helicopter was a battered heap, lying on its side, flames rising all around.

Gunning the throttle, Emma sped across the prairie, praying she wasn't too late. Maybe the pilot had been thrown clear of the aircraft. She hoped she was right.

As she neared the wreck, movement caught her attention. Another snowmobile was headed toward the helicopter from the north. *Good,* she thought. Maybe whoever it was had also seen the chopper crash and could help her free the pilot from the wreckage and get him to safety. She waved her hand, hoping the driver would see her and know she was there to help. He didn't give any indication he'd spotted her. But the snowmobile slowed. The rider pulled off his helmet, his dark head in sharp contrast to his white jacket. He leveled what appeared to be a rifle across the handlebars, aiming at something near the wall of flames.

Emma squinted, trying to make out what he was doing. The pop of rifle fire made her jump. That's when she noticed a dark lump on the ground in the snow, outside the ring of fire around the helicopter. The lump moved, rolling over in the snow.

The driver of the other snowmobile climbed onto the vehicle and started toward the man on the ground, moving slowly, his rifle poised to shoot.

Emma gasped.

The man was trying to shoot the guy on the ground.

With a quick twist of the throttle she sent her snowmobile skimming across the snow, headed straight for the attacker. At the angle she was traveling, the attacker wouldn't see her if he was concentrating on the man on the ground.

Unarmed, she only had her snowmobile and her wits. The man on the ground only had one chance at survival. If she didn't get to him or the other snowmobile first, he didn't stand a chance.

Coming in from the west, Emma aimed for the man with the gun. She didn't have a plan other than to ram him and hope for the best.

He didn't see her or hear her engine over the roar of his own until she was within twenty feet of him. The man turned the weapon toward her.

Emma gave the engine all it could take and raced straight for the man. He fired a shot. Something plinked against the hood of the snowmobile engine. At the last moment, she turned the handlebars. Her machine slid into the side of his and the handlebars knocked the gun from his hand.

She twisted the throttle and skidded sideways across the snow, spinning around to face him again.

Disarmed, the attacker had turned as well and raced north, away from the burning helicopter and the man on the ground.

Emma watched as the snowmobile continued into the distance. Keeping an eye on the north, she turned her snowmobile south toward the figure lying still on the ground.

She pulled up beside him and leaped off the snowmobile into the packed snow where he'd rolled.

A man in thermal underwear lay facedown in the snow, blood oozing from his left arm, dripping bright red against the pristine white snow.

Emma bent toward him, her hand reaching out to push him over.

The man moved so quickly, she didn't know what hit her. He rolled over, snatched her wrist and jerked her flat onto her belly, then straddled her, his knees planted on both sides of her hips, twisting her arm up between her shoulder blades.

Until that point, she hadn't realized just how vulnerable she was. On the snowmobile, she had a way to escape. Once she'd left the vehicle, she'd put herself at risk. What if the man shooting had been the good guy? In the middle of nowhere, with a big man towering over her, she was trapped and out of ideas.

"Let me up!" she yelled, aiming for righteous contempt. Her voice wobbled, muffled by a mouthful of snow it sounded more like a frog's croak.

She tried to twist around to face him, but he planted his fist into the middle of her back, holding her down, the cold snow biting her cheek.

"Why did you shoot down my helicopter?" he demanded, his voice rough but oddly familiar.

"I didn't, you big baboon," she insisted. "The other guy did."

His hands roved over her body, patting her sides, hips, buttocks, legs and finally slipping beneath her jacket and up to her breasts. His hands froze there and she swore.

Emma spit snow and shouted, "Hey! Hands off!"

As quickly as she'd been face-planted in the snow, the man on top of her flipped her onto her back and stared down at her with his dark green eyes.

"Dante?"

"Emma?" He shook his head. "What the hell are you doing here?"

# Chapter Two

"Well, I'm sure not on a picnic," Emma said, her voice dripping with sarcasm.

Dante stared down at the pretty young college professor he'd met when he'd taken classes at the University of North Dakota, working toward a master's degree in operations management.

She stared up at him with warm, dark chocolate-colored eyes, her gaze scanning his face. "What happened to you?" She reached up to touch his temple, her fingers coming away with blood. "Why was that man shooting at you?"

"I don't know." Dante's brow furrowed. "Did you get a good look at him?"

"No, it was all a blur. I thought he was coming to help, but then he started shooting at you. I rammed into him, knocking his gun out of his hands. Then he took off."

"You shouldn't have put yourself in that kind of danger."

"What was I supposed to do, stand by and watch him kill you?"

"Thankfully, he didn't shoot *you*. And thanks for saving my butt." Dante staggered to his feet and reached down with his right hand and helped her up. "He shot down my helicopter with an RPG and would have finished me off if you hadn't come along." A bitterly cold,

Arctic breeze rippled across the prairie, blowing straight through his thermal underwear. A shiver racked his body and he gritted his teeth to keep them from chattering.

Emma stood and brushed the snow off her pants and jacket. "What happened to your clothes?"

"I fell into a puddle of flaming aviation fuel when I climbed out of the helicopter." He glanced back at the inferno. "We need to get out of here in case the fire ignites the fuel in the tank."

He climbed onto her snowmobile.

"You should take my coat. I bet you're freezing." Emma started to unzip her jacket.

He held up his hand. "Don't. I can handle it for a little while and no use in both of us being cold." He moved back on the seat and tipped his head. "Get on. I don't know where you came from, but I hope it's warmer there than it is here."

Her lips twisted, but she didn't waste time. She slipped her leg over the seat and pressed the start button. She prayed the bent skid, damaged in the collision, wouldn't slow them down.

Once she was aboard, Dante wrapped his arms around her and pressed his body against her back, letting her body block some of the bitter wind.

It wasn't enough. The cold went right through his underwear, biting at his skin. He started shaking before they'd gone twenty yards. By the time they topped a rise, he could no longer feel his fingers.

Emma drove the snowmobile along a ridge below which a tent poked up out of the snow. A truck and trailer stood on the ridge, looking to Dante like heaven.

When she pulled up beside the trailer, Emma climbed off, looped one of Dante's arms over her shoulder and helped him into the trailer. It wasn't much warmer inside, but the wind was blocked and for that Dante could be very grateful. The trailer consisted of a bed, a sink, a small refrigerator and a tiny bathroom.

"Sit." Emma pushed him onto the bed, pulled off his boots and shoved his legs under the goose down blanket and a number of well-worn quilts. She handed him a dry washcloth. "Hold this on your shoulder so you don't bleed all over everything."

"Yes, ma'am," he said with a smile.

Her brows dipped. "Stay here while I get the generator running." She opened the door, letting in a cold blast of air.

"Keep your eyes open," he said through chattering teeth.

"I will." She closed the door behind her and the room was silent.

Dante hunkered down into the blankets, feeling as though he should be the one out there stirring the generator to life. When Emma hadn't returned in five minutes, he pushed the blankets aside, wrapped one around himself and went looking for her.

He was reaching for the doorknob when the door jerked open.

Emma frowned up at him, her dark hair dusted in snowflakes. "The generator's not working."

"Let me look at it," he insisted.

She pushed past him, closing the door behind her. "It won't do any good."

"Why?"

"The fuel line is busted." She held up the offending tube and waved him toward the bed. "Get back under the covers. At least we have a gas stove we can use to warm it up a little in here. I don't recommend running it all night, but it'll do for now."

"Why don't we get out of here?"

"It's almost dark and it started snowing pretty hard, I can barely see my hand in front of my face. It's hard enough to find my way out here in daylight. I'm not trying in the dark and especially not in North Dakota blizzard conditions."

"I need to let the base know what happened." He glanced around. "Do you have any kind of radio or cell phone?"

"I have a cell phone, but it won't work out here." She shrugged. "No towers nearby."

His body shook, his head ached and his vision was hazy. "I need to get back."

"Tomorrow. Now go back to bed before you fall down. I'm strong, but not strong enough to pick up a big guy like you."

Dante let Emma guide him back to the bed and tuck him in. When she smoothed the blankets over his chest, he grabbed her hand.

Her gaze met his as he carried her hand to his lips and kissed the back of her knuckles. "Thanks for saving my life."

Her cheeks reddened and she looked away. "You'd have done the same."

"I doubt seriously you'd be shot down from the sky. Your feet are pretty firmly on the ground." He smiled. "Paleontologist, right?"

She nodded.

"Isn't it a little late in the season to be at a dig? I thought they shut them down when the fall session started."

She shrugged. "With our unseasonably warm weather, I've been working this dig every weekend since the semester started."

"Until recently."

"Since it snowed a few days ago, I figured I'd better get out here. I'd heard more snow was coming, and I needed to dismantle my tent and bring it in." She stared toward the window as if she could see through the blinding snow.

"I take it you didn't get the tent down in time."

She gave him a little crooked smile. "A downed helicopter distracted me."

"Well, thank you for sacrificing your tent to be a Good Samaritan."

Her cheeks reddened and she turned away. "Let's get that shoulder cleaned up and bandaged."

She wet a cloth and returned to the bedside. Pushing the fabric of his thermal shirt aside, she washed the blood away.

Her fingers were gentle around the gash.

"It's just a scratch."

Her lips quirked. When she'd washed away the drying blood, she applied an antiseptic ointment and a bandage. "As it is, it was just a flesh wound, but it wouldn't do to get infected." Patting the bandage, she stepped back, the color higher in her cheeks. "I'll make you a cup of hot tea, if you'd like."

Studying her face, Dante found he liked the way she blushed so easily. "Have any coffee?"

"Sorry. I didn't expect to have guests."

"In that case, tea would be nice." Dante glanced around the tiny confines of the trailer. "Aren't you afraid to come out to places like this alone?"

Emma reached for two mugs from a cabinet. "Why should I be? It's not like anyone else comes out here."

"What if you were to get hurt?"

She shrugged. "It's a chance I'm willing to take."

"As close as it is to the border, you might be subject to more than just an elk hunter or farmer."

"I have a gun." Emma opened a drawer and pulled out a long, vintage revolver.

Dante grinned. "You call that a gun?"

She stiffened. "I certainly do."

"It's an antique."

"A Colt .45 caliber, Single Action Army revolver, to be exact."

Nodding, impressed, Dante stated, "You know the name of your antiques."

Her chin tipped upward. "And I'm an expert shot."

"My apologies for doubting you."

The wind picked up outside, rocking the tiny trailer on its wheels.

Emma struck a long kitchen match on the side of a box and lit one of the two burners on the stove. A bright flame cast a rosy glow in the quickly darkening space. She filled a teakettle with water from a large water bottle and settled it over the flame. "I have canned chili, canned tuna and crackers. Again, I hadn't planned on staying more than a couple of nights. I was supposed to head out before the weather laid in."

Despite his injuries, Dante's stomach grumbled. "I don't want to take your food."

She leveled her gaze at him. "I wouldn't offer if I didn't have enough."

"Then, thank you."

She opened two cans of chili and poured them into a pot, lit the other burner and settled the food over the flame.

Before long the teakettle steamed and the rich aroma of tomato sauce and chili powder filled the air. Emma moved with grace and efficiency, the gentle swell of her hips swaying from side to side as she moved between the sink and the stove. Dante's groin tightened. Not that she was his typical type.

Emma appeared to be straitlaced and uptight with little time in her agenda for playing the field, as proved by their one date that had gone nowhere. Still, it didn't give him the right to go after her again.

He shoved aside the blanket and tried to stand. "I should be helping you." A chill hit him, penetrating his long underwear as if he wore nothing at all.

"Stay put." She waved in his direction. "There's little enough room in the trailer without two people bumping into each other. And I've got this covered." She shed her jacket and hung it on a hook on the wall.

"I can at least get the plates and utensils down and set the table." He glanced around. "Uh, where is the table?"

Emma grinned. "It's under the bed. You were lying on it."

He gave her a half bow. "Where do you propose we eat?"

"On the bed." She grinned. "Picnic-style."

"Do you always eat in the bed?" Images of the slightly stiff Emma wearing a baby-doll nightgown, sitting on the coverlet, eating chocolate-covered strawberries popped into Dante's head. He tried but failed to banish the thought, his groin tightening even more. The slim professor with the chocolate-brown hair and eyes, and luscious lips tempted the saint right out of him. And the kicker was that she didn't even know she was so very hot.

"I don't usually have company in my trailer. I can eat wherever I want. In the summertime, I sit on a camp stool outside and watch the sun set over the dig."

He could picture the brilliant red, orange and mauve skies tinting her hair. "I'll consider it an adventure." He reached around her and opened one of the overhead cabinet doors. "Where are the dishes and utensils?" As he leaned over her, the scent of roses tantalized his nostrils. Her hair shone in the light from the flame on the stove as much as he thought it might in the dying embers of a North Dakota sunset. Despite having shed her coat, the thick sweater, turtleneck and snow pants hid most of her shape. But he could remember it from the class he'd audited while attending the university in Grand Forks.

He tucked a hair behind her ear. "Why was it we only went out once?"

Her head dipped. "One has to ask for a second date."

Dante gripped her shoulders gently and turned her slowly toward him. "I didn't call, did I?" He stared down at her until she glanced up.

Her lips twisted. "It's no big deal. We only went out for coffee."

Dante swallowed hard. He remembered. It had been shortly before a particularly harsh bout of depression. One of his buddies from the army had been shot down in Afghanistan. He'd wondered if he'd stayed in the army if he could have changed the course of events, perhaps saved his friend or if he would have died in his place. Losing his fiancée and his friend so soon afterward made him question everything he'd thought he'd understood—his role in the war on terrorism, his patriotism and his faith in mankind. It had been all he could do to get out of bed each morning, go to work and fly the border missions.

"I'm sorry." He brushed a thumb across her full lower lip and then bent to follow his thumb with his mouth. He'd only meant to kiss her softly, but once his lips touched hers, he couldn't stop himself. A rush of hunger like he'd never known washed over him and before he realized it, he was crushing her mouth, his tongue darting out to take hers.

When he raised his head, he stared down at her through a haze of lust, wanting to drag her across the bed and strip her of every layer of clothing.

Her big brown eyes were wide, her lips swollen from his kiss and pink flags of color stained her cheeks.

Dante closed his eyes, forcing himself to be reasonable and controlled. "I'm sorry. I shouldn't have done that."

"I don't—" she started.

The teakettle whistled.

Emma jerked around to the stove, one hand going to the handle of the kettle, the other to her lips.

Dante retrieved bowls from the cabinet and spoons from a drawer and stepped back, giving her as much space as the interior of the trailer would allow.

The wind churned outside, wailing against the flimsy outer walls, the cold seeping through.

As she poured the water into the mugs, Emma's hand shook.

Kicking himself for his impulsive act, Dante vowed to keep his hands—and lips—to himself for the duration of their confinement in the tight space.

Since resigning his commission, Dante hadn't considered himself fit for any relationship. He'd come back to North Dakota, hoping to reclaim the life he'd known growing up. But the transition from soldier to civilian had been anything but easy. Every loud noise made him duck, expecting incoming rounds from hidden enemies. Until today, it had only been noise. Today he'd been under attack and he hadn't been prepared.

Emma dipped a tea bag in each mug until the water turned the desired shade. Then she pulled the bags out and set them in the tiny sink. "I'm sorry, I don't have milk or lemon." She held out a mug to him. "Sugar?"

The way her lips moved to say that one word had him ready to break his recent vow. "No, I'll take it straight."

When she handed him the mug, their hands touched and an electric surge zipped through him. He backed away and his knees bumped into the mattress, forcing him to sit and slosh hot tea on his hand. The scalding liquid brought him back to his senses.

Emma spooned chili into bowls and handed one to him. "Who would shoot you out of the sky?" She cradled her bowl in both hands, blowing the steam off the top.

"I have no idea."

"As a border patrol agent, have you pissed off anyone lately?"

He shook his head. "Not anyone who would have the firepower that man had. He used a Soviet-made RPG from what I could tell. How the hell he got ahold of one of those, I don't know."

"How'd he know you'd be here?"

"I was responding to a call from my base that a man had crossed the U.S.-Canadian border on a snowmobile in this area. I can only assume it was him."

"Could be someone with a gripe against the border patrol."

"Yeah. I wish I could get word to my supervisor. They'll be freaking out right about now. A missing helicopter and pilot is a big deal."

"Would they send out a rescue team?"

"In this weather, I don't see how."

"Hopefully, it'll be gone in the morning." She stirred her chili. "If they don't come looking for you, we'll do our best to drive out and find a farmer with a landline so that you can call back."

He nodded. "A lot of people will be worried. That's an expensive piece of equipment to lose."

"Seems to me that a skilled pilot is harder to replace." Emma took a bite of her chili and chewed slowly.

Dante shrugged. Everything would have to wait until tomorrow. In the meantime… "It's getting colder outside."

"I have plenty of blankets for one bed." She stared at her empty bowl and a shiver shook her body. "Without the generator, we'll have to share the warmth." Her gaze clashed with his, hers appearing reserved, wary.

His lips thinning, Dante raised his hands. "I'm sorry about the kiss. I promise to keep my hands to myself."

Before he finished talking, Emma was shaking her head. "It's going to get really cold, The only way to stay warm is to stay close and share body warmth."

Dante swallowed hard, his body warming at the thought.

He set his empty chili bowl in the sink and took hers from her, laying it on top. "We're adults. This doesn't have to be awkward or a big deal," he said while his body was telling him, *Oh, yes it does!*

## Chapter Three

Emma stared at the bed, her heart thumping against her ribs, her mouth going bone-dry. If it wasn't so darned cold in the trailer, she'd sit up all night on the camp stool.

No, she wasn't afraid of Dante. Frankly, she was afraid of her body's reaction to being so close to the tall, dark Native American.

Too awkward around the opposite sex in high school, she'd focused instead on excelling in her studies. While girls her age were kissing beneath the bleachers, she was playing the French horn in band and counting the minutes until she could go back home to her books.

College had been little better. At least her freshman roommate in the dorm had seen some potential in her and shown her how to dress and do her hair and makeup. She'd even set her up on a blind date, which had ended woefully short when she had yanked her hand out of his when he'd tried to hold it.

For all her schooling, she was remarkably unschooled in the ways of love.

The wind moaned outside, sending a frigid chill raking across her body. Her hands shaking, she pushed the snow pants down over her hips and sat on the side of the bed to pull off her boots, slipping the pants off with them. Then she slid beneath the covers in her thermal underwear, sweater and turtleneck shirt and scooted all the way to the other side of the small mattress.

What man could lust after a woman covered from neck to feet? Not that she wanted him to lust after her. What would she do? Heaven help her if he should find out she was a virgin at the ripe old age of twenty-six.

Emma lay on her back, the blankets pulled up to her chin and her eyes wide in the dim glow of the stove's fire. "You'll need to turn off the flame before we go to sleep." Perhaps in the dark she'd felt less conspicuous and self-conscious.

Dante reached for the knob on the little stove and switched it off. The flame disappeared, throwing them into complete darkness.

The blanket tugged against her death grip, and the mattress sank beneath the big man's weight. "Don't worry. I promise not to touch you."

*Damn,* Emma thought. With a man as gorgeous as Dante Thunder Horse lying next to her, what if she wanted him to touch her? Then again, one close encounter with her bumbling, shy inexperienced self and he'd disappear, just like he had the last time she'd gotten up the courage to go out for coffee with him.

He stretched out alongside her, his shoulder and thigh bumping against her.

A ripple of anticipation fluttered through her belly, followed by a bone-rattling shiver as the cold seeped through the three blankets, her sweater and thermal underwear.

"This is foolish. We won't last the night in the frigid cold without heat." He turned on his side and reached around her.

"W-what are you doing?" she squeaked as his hand brushed across her breast.

"We're both fully clothed, which, by the way, isn't helping matters. We're both adults and we're freezing. The best way to warm up is to share heat."

"That's what we were doing."

"Not like this." He rolled her onto her side, pulled her against him and spooned her backside with his front, his arm draped around her middle. "Better?"

Her pulse pounded so loud she could barely hear him, but she nodded and whispered, "Better." Far too much better.

As she lay in the dark, cocooned in blankets and a handsome man's arms, part of her was freaking out, the other part was shouting inside, *Hallelujah!*

"Let's go to sleep and hopefully the storm will have passed by morning."

Sleep? Was he kidding? Every cell in her body was firing up, while her core was in meltdown stages. Little shivers of excitement ignited beneath her skin with his every movement. His warm breath stirred the tendrils of hair lying against the side of her throat and all she could think of was how close his lips were to her neck. How likely was he to repeat the kiss that happened just a few moments ago?

If she turned over and faced him, would he feel compelled to repeat the performance? Did she dare?

"You smell nice. Like roses." His chest rumbled against her back, his arm tightening around her middle.

"Must be my shampoo. It was a gift from a friend." As soon as she said it, she could have kicked herself. Why couldn't she just say *thank you* like any other woman paid a compliment?

"Am I making you nervous?" he asked.

"I'm not used to having a man…spoon me."

"Seriously?" His thighs pressed against the backs of

her legs and one slid across hers. "They were missing out. You're very spoonable."

She bit her bottom lip, afraid to admit she was a failure at relationships and scared off the men who'd ever made an attempt to get to know her. "I'm not good at this."

"It's as natural as breathing," he said, his big hand spanning her belly. "Speaking of which, just breathe," he whispered against her ear.

His words had the opposite effect, causing her breath to lodge in her throat, her heart to stop for a full second and then race to catch up.

Her arm lay over his and she wasn't sure what to do with her hand. When she let it relax, it fell across his big, warm one.

"Your fingers are so cold," he said.

She jerked her hand back. "I'm sorry."

"Don't be. Let me have them." He felt along her arm until he located her hand and enveloped it in his. "Tuck it beneath your shirt, like this." He slipped his hand with hers under the hems of her sweater and thermal shirt, placing them against the heat of her skin. "You're as stiff as a board. Are you still cold?" He moved his body closer.

"Yes," she lied. Inside she was on fire, her nerve synapses firing off each time he bumped against her.

His fingers curled around hers, his knuckles brushing against her belly. "You really haven't ever snuggled with a man?"

Not trusting her voice, she shook her head.

"Then you haven't found the right one." Dante's lips brushed the curl of her ear.

She lay for a while basking in the closeness, letting her senses get used to the idea of him being so near, so intimate.

Without the heat from the stove top, the trailer's

interior became steadily colder and Dante's hand holding hers inched upward beneath her shirt. "Just tell me if you want me to stop."

*Oh, heck no.* If anything, she wanted him to move faster and cup her breasts with that big, warm hand. A shiver of excitement shook her.

"Still cold?"

"Yes." So it was a half truth. The parts of her body against his were warm, the others were cold and getting colder.

"Sharing body heat works better when you're skin to skin." His knuckles nudged the swells of her breasts.

Her breath caught in her throat when she said, "I know." Emma bit her bottom lip, wondering if Dante would take her words as an invitation to initiate the next move.

"I don't know about you, but it's getting pretty damn cold in here. If we want to keep warm all night, we'd better do what it takes." He removed his hand from her belly and rolled onto his back.

The cold enveloped her immediately and she scooted over to lie on her back as well, tugging the blanket up to her nose.

Dante sat up next to her, tugging the blanket aside, letting even colder air beneath.

"What are you doing?" she said through chattering teeth.

"Getting naked." His movements indicated he was removing his thermal shirt and stuffing it beneath the covers down near his feet. He slid his long underwear over his hips, his hands bumping into her thigh as he pushed them all the way down to his feet.

"Now your turn." He reached for the hem of her sweater and dragged it over her head.

"Are you crazy? It's f-freezing in here." She tried to keep her turtleneck shirt on, but he was as determined to remove that as he'd been with the sweater.

"Again, we're adults. If it helps, just think of me as a big electric blanket to wrap around you." He stuffed her shirt and sweater into the space around her feet and went to work on the long thermal underwear, dragging them down over her legs.

By the time he had her stripped to her bra and panties, she was shaking uncontrollably. "I was w-warmer b-before you s-started," she said through chattering teeth.

"You'll be warm again. Come here." He dragged the blanket over them and pulled her close, crushing her breasts against his chest, his big arms wrapping around her back, tucking the blanket in as close as he could get it.

Their breath mingled, the heat of their skin, touching everywhere but her bra and panties, helped to chase away the chills. But Emma still couldn't stop shaking. She'd never lain nearly naked with a man. She had trouble breathing and couldn't figure out where her hands were supposed to be. Planting them against his chest was putting too much space between them and allowing cold air to keep her front chilled. She tried moving them down to her side, but her fingers were cold and she wanted them warm. When she slipped them around to her belly, they bumped against a hot, stiff shaft.

As soon as she touched it, she realized it was his member and before she could think, her hands wrapped around it.

"Baby, only go there if you mean it," he warned her. "As close and naked as we are, it wouldn't take much to set me off."

"I thought you were just an electric blanket," she whispered, reveling in a surge of power rolling through her.

She had caused him to be this way. Her body against his was making him desire her in a way she'd only dreamed about.

For a moment, all her awkward insecurities disappeared. Her fingers tightened around him and slid downward to the base of his shaft.

His arms squeezed around her and his hips rocked, pressing himself into her grip.

Blood hummed through her veins. For that moment, she forgot the chill in the air and the fact they could freeze to death. Her focus centered on what she had in her hands and, in connection, what it could lead to.

Dante moaned. "Do you know what you're doing to me?"

"I think so," she responded. Her hand glided up his shaft to the velvety tip, her core heating, liquid fire swirling at her center, readying her to take him.

"I didn't get us naked in order to take advantage of you."

Her hands froze. "Am I taking advantage of *you?*"

"Oh, hell no."

Her finger swirled across the tip, memorizing him by touch. "Just say so and I'll stop," she repeated his words.

"Are you sure you want to do this?" He ran his hands over her back and down to smooth over her bottom.

She laughed, emboldened by the complete darkness. "I've never been more sure of anything in my life." Something about the anonymity of the dark gave her the confidence to continue. Then she hesitated. "Unless you don't want to. You're the injured party."

"I've wanted this since I stole that kiss." He hooked the elastic of her panties and slid them down her legs.

She kicked them off, loving the way his member

pressed into her curly mound. Just a little lower and he'd be there.

"I don't have protection," he said.

"I'm clean of STDs if that's what you're saying." How could she not be when she'd never made love to a man?

"So am I." He nuzzled her neck, his lips pressing against her pounding pulse. "But we shouldn't do this without protection."

"Can't you withdraw at the last minute?"

"Withdrawal isn't one-hundred percent safe."

"You can't stop now." Surely she couldn't get pregnant on her first time. Her first time. Wow. With a man as gorgeous and gentle as Dante, maybe she'd finally overcome her awkward shyness. She trembled, her body shaking like an engine when it first starts.

"Are we going to do it?" she asked, her hand tugging on him, guiding him to her center.

He chuckled softly. "Say the word."

She inhaled and let out the single word on a breath of air, "Please."

Dante hesitated for less than a second, and then he rolled on top of her, nudged her legs apart with his knees and settled between her thighs, his member pressing to her opening.

But he didn't enter, not immediately. He started with a kiss. One similar to the one he'd stolen at the stove. This time, Emma kissed him back, finding his tongue and sliding hers along the length of his. She curled her fingers around the back of his neck and dragged him closer, loving the feel of his smooth chest against her fingers. She reached behind her and unclasped her bra, wanting her naked breasts to feel what her fingers had the pleasure of.

Dante tore it away and slid it beneath her pillow, then he pulled the blanket over their heads and moved down her body. Inch by inch, he tasted her with his tongue, nipping her with his teeth, settling first on one breast, sucking the tip into his mouth and rolling the tight bud around. He moved to the other and gave it equal attention before he inched lower, skimming across her ribs and down past her belly button to the tuft of hair at the apex of her thighs.

Emma held her breath, wondering what he would do next. His mouth so close to home, she couldn't move, frozen to the sheets, waiting.

With his big, rough fingers, he parted her folds and stroked that sensitive strip of skin.

"Oh, my!" she exclaimed, her heels digging into the mattress, raising her hips for more.

He swirled, tapped and flicked, setting her world on fire. When she thought she couldn't take any more, he moved up her body, and pressed into her.

At the barrier of her virginity, he paused.

Emma wrapped her legs around his waist and dug her heels into his buttocks, urging him deeper. "Don't stop," she pleaded.

"But…"

"Just do it. Please." She tightened her legs.

He thrust deeper, tearing through.

She must have gasped, because he pulled back a little. "Are you all right?" Dante asked.

She laughed shakily. "I'd be better if you didn't stop."

After hesitating a moment longer, he slid slowly into her and began a steady, easy glide in and out.

The initial pain lasted but a moment, and soon Emma forgot it in the joy of the connection between them. So this was what all the fuss was about. Now she understood and dropped her feet to the mattress to better meet him thrust for thrust.

When Dante stiffened, he stopped, his hard member buried deep inside her. A moment later, he dragged himself free and lay down beside her, pulling her into the warmth of his arms.

The heat of his body and the haze of pleasurable exhaustion washed over her and she melted against him. "Mmm. I never knew it would be that good."

He lay with his arms around her, his body stiff. "You cried out. Why?"

Heat rose into her cheeks. "Did I?"

For a long moment, Dante held her without talking. "You were a virgin, weren't you?" When she refused to answer, he continued, "Why didn't you tell me?"

Emma rested her hand on his chest, feeling the swift beat of his heart against her palm. "I was embarrassed. Besides, what difference does it make?"

"We wouldn't have done it." He smoothed a hand along her lower back.

"Are you sorry you did?" she asked, her lips so close to his nipple, she tongued the hard little point, liking the way it beaded even tighter.

"No."

She smiled in the darkness and relaxed against him. "Me, either. Virginity is way overrated."

He tipped her chin up with his finger. "Then why are—*were*—you still one?" His breath warmed her.

"Like I told you. I'm not good at relationships. I could never get past a first date."

She could feel his head shaking side to side. "Inconceivable," he said, then captured her mouth with his.

When he broke the kiss, Emma lay in his arms, basking in the afterglow, their bodies generating enough combined heat that, along with the cocoon of blankets, they held off the cold.

"Just so you know, I'm not good at relationships, either," Dante said into the darkness. "I can offer you no guarantees."

"I understand." The warmth she'd been feeling chilled slightly. What did she expect? Sex was sex. No matter how good it felt, it didn't necessarily come with emotional commitment.

She couldn't expect Dante to fall in love with her just because she'd given him her virginity. "Don't worry. I won't stalk you or make any demands of you. The 'no guarantees' thing goes both ways."

His hand paused the circular motion he'd begun on her naked back.

She added to boost her own self-confidence, "Thank you for getting me over my awkwardness. I won't be so hesitant with my future dates." As soon as she said the words, she could have kicked herself. Would he consider them flippant and insensitive, or worse? Would he think she was loose and easy with her body?

Despite his announcement that he'd give no guarantees, she'd harbored a wish, a dream and a raging desire to repeat what had just happened. When the storm cleared and they made it back to civilization, she hoped he'd ask her out again. Though sex with Dante had been magical to her, he certainly wouldn't be impressed enough for a repeat performance with an awkward ex-virgin?

# Chapter Four

*Dante pressed himself as close as he could get to the jagged hulk of his crashed helicopter; his copilot lay at an awkward angle, still strapped to his seat, dead from a broken neck sustained upon impact. He didn't recognize the copilot, his face was hidden in shadows.*

*A movement at the edge of the village where he'd crashed caught Dante's eye. The flap of a dark robe fluttered in the desert breeze. There. The man he'd seen at the last minute, pointing an RPG at him, stood at the corner of a mud hut.*

*Staying low behind the metal wreckage, Dante leveled his 9 mm pistol, aiming at the man, waiting for him to step out of the shadows and come within range.*

*The sound of an engine made his blood run cold. An old, rusty truck rumbled down the middle of the street between the buildings, loaded with Taliban soldiers wielding Soviet-made rifles.*

*Alone, without any backup, it was him with a full clip against the Taliban. If he wanted to live, he had to make every shot count.*

*The truck barreled toward him and stopped short. The soldiers leaped over the side. He fired, hitting one, then another, but they kept coming as if the truck had an endless supply. One by one, he fired until the trigger clicked and the clip was empty.*

*Taliban men grabbed his arms and pulled him from the wreckage, shouting and shooting their weapons in the air. The hum of the truck engine growled louder as they dragged him closer.*

"Dante."

*How did they know his name? He struggled against their hold, kicking and shoving at their hands.*

"Dante, wake up!"

He opened his eyes. The sand and desert disappeared and dim light seeped in around the blinds over a window.

"Dante?" a soft feminine voice called out and it all came back to him.

"Emma?" he said, his voice hoarse.

She leaned over him, her naked body pressed against his, her breasts smashed to his chest, her thigh draped over his. She smelled of roses mixed with the musky scent of sex.

It took him a moment to shake the terror of being captured and dragged away by the Taliban, and even longer to return to the camp trailer on the North Dakota tundra.

Then he noticed a red mark on Emma's cheek. "What happened to you?" He reached up to gently brush his thumb around the mark.

She smiled crookedly. "You were having a bad dream."

"I did that?" His chest tightened and he pushed to a sitting position. "Oh, Emma, I'm so sorry."

"It doesn't hurt." She pressed her fingers to the red welt. "I'm more worried about the engine noise I hear outside."

Dante sat still and silent, focusing on the noise from outside. Just as she'd said, an engine revved nearby.

Dante threw back the covers. "Get up. Get dressed."

"Why?" She asked, scrambling off the bed, gooseflesh rising on her naked skin.

"We don't know if the man who shot me down yesterday is back."

"Damn." Emma grabbed her sweater, tugged it over her naked breasts and slipped into her snow pants and boots.

Dante only had his thermals to pull on and his boots.

When he reached for the door handle and twisted, it didn't open. "Is there some kind of lock on this?"

"It should open when you twist the handle."

He tried again.

About that time, the trailer lurched, sending him flying across the floor, slamming into the sink.

Emma fell across the bed. "What the hell?"

"The door lock is jammed, and someone's driving your truck with the trailer still attached. Hold on!"

The vehicle lurched and bumped over the rough terrain.

"He's backing us up!" Emma shouted. "If he goes much farther, we'll end up in the ditch my team has been digging." She staggered to her feet and flung herself across the room to the door. Another bump and her forehead slammed into the wall.

She slipped, her hands grabbing for the door latch. "We have to stop him."

Dante staggered across to her. "Move!" He picked her up and shoved her to the side. Bracing himself on whatever he could hold on to, he slammed his heel into the door. The force with which he hit reverberated up his leg. The door remained secure. He kicked again. Nothing.

Emma grasped the sink and ripped the blinds from the window. "Oh, my god. We're going to fall—"

The trailer tipped wildly. Everything that wasn't nailed to the floor, including Dante and Emma, was flung to the back of the trailer as it tumbled down the near-vertical slope of the dig site. The rear end of the trailer slammed into the ground, crumpling on impact. Cold air blasted through the cracks and glass broke from the windows.

Dante landed on the mattress as it slid toward the back of the trailer. "Emma?" He couldn't see her anywhere.

"I'm okay, I think." A hand waved from beneath the mattress. "I'm just stuck."

The truck engine revved and a door slammed outside. Then the upper end of the trailer caved in, bearing down on them. Dante rolled to the side, letting the mattress take the bulk of the blow.

When the world quit shaking, Dante was jammed between the mattress and the wall. Metal squeaked against metal and the trailer seemed to groan.

"Dante?" Emma called out.

"I'm going to try to move this mattress." He squeezed himself against the wall and rolled the mattress back. "Can you get yourself out?"

"I'll try." Emma reached up, grabbed the edge of the sink and pulled herself out from beneath the mattress.

Dante let the mattress fall in place and hauled himself up on it, ducking low to keep from hitting his head on the crushed trailer. His stomach lurched when he saw the bumper of the truck through a crack in the wall. Whoever had driven them into the ditch had crashed the truck down on top of them. If it shifted even a little, they'd be stuck in there, trapped and possibly crushed.

Light and cold wind filtered through the broken window over the sink. Placing his head close to the opening, he listened.

"Is he gone?" Emma whispered.

A small engine roared above them. If he wasn't mistaken, Dante would guess it was a snowmobile. "I think that's him leaving now." And none too soon. The truck above them shifted and the walls sank closer to where he and Emma crouched on the mattress.

The door was crushed and mangled. They wouldn't be getting out that way. If they didn't leave soon, the truck would smash into them. "We have to get out of here."

"How?" Emma asked.

Dante lay back and kicked the rest of the glass out of the window over the sink. Then, using the pillow, he worked the jagged edges loose. "You go first," he said.

"And leave you to be crushed?" Emma shook her head. "No way. If you can get out, I can get out."

"If I get stuck, neither one of us will get out. If you go first and I'm trapped, you can go for help."

Emma worried her bottom lip between her teeth. "Okay. But you're not getting stuck." She edged her body through the tight opening and dropped to the ground. "Now you!" she called out. "And throw any blankets or coats you can salvage out with you."

Dante scavenged two blankets from the rubble and pushed them through the window. He followed them with Emma's winter jacket.

Metal shrieked against metal and the trailer's walls quaked.

"The truck's shifting!" Emma called out. "Get out now!"

Dante dove for the small window, wondering how he'd get his broad shoulders through the narrow opening. He squeezed one through and angled the other, the rim of the window tight around his ribs. Then he was pushing himself through.

Emma braced his hands on her shoulders and walked backward as he brought his hips and legs almost all the way out.

The entire structure wobbled and creaked, then folded like an accordion.

Emma dragged him the rest of the way, both of them falling onto the ground as the truck's weight crushed the remainder of the trailer walls beneath it.

Dante rolled off Emma and stood, pulling her up beside him. Together they stared at the wreckage.

She shook in the curve of his arm. "If one more minute had passed…"

His arm tightened around her. "We're out. That's all that matters."

"But who would do this?"

"I don't know, but I'm sure as hell going to find out."

EMMA COULDN'T REMEMBER the road leading into the dig site being as long as it was, until she had to walk through snow to get to a paved road. Her toes were frozen and her jacket barely kept the cold wind from chilling her body to the bone. But she couldn't complain when all Dante had on were his thermal underwear and the blankets he'd salvaged from the trailer before it had been crushed beneath her truck.

With the truck a total write-off, she'd hoped the snowmobile she'd left parked outside the night before would be usable.

Whoever had tried to kill them had stabbed a hole in the snowmobile's gas tank and ripped the wires loose. It wasn't going anywhere but a junkyard.

If they wanted to get help, they were forced to trudge through three feet of snow for almost two miles just to reach a paved road. And as the North Dakota countryside could be desolate, it could be hours or days before anyone passed by on the paved road.

Tired, hungry and cold, Emma formed a smile with her chapped lips. At least she wouldn't die a virgin. "Are you doing okay?" she asked. "We could stop and hunker down long enough for you to warm up."

"I'm fine." Enveloped in the two blankets he'd thrown from the wreckage, his thermal-clad legs were more exposed to the elements than anything else. "We should keep moving."

Emma could tell he was trying not to let his teeth chatter. She slipped her arm around him and leaned her body into his to block as much of the wind as she could. Blankets provided little protection against the icy Arctic winds. If they didn't find help soon, he'd freeze to death. How much could a man persevere after being shot down and nearly crushed?

Her gaze swept over him. The man, all muscle and strength, displayed no weakness. But as cold as she was, he had to be freezing.

Though the storm had moved on and the sun had come out, the wind hadn't let up, seeming to come directly from the North Pole.

When they reached pavement, Emma almost felt giddy with relief. With the gravel road she'd come in on buried in snow, she hadn't been completely sure they were headed in the right direction.

"Which way?" Dante asked.

Emma glanced right, then left, and back right again. "If I recall correctly, the man who owns this ranch lives in a house a couple of miles north of this turnoff."

A cold blast of wind sent a violent shiver across her body.

"Here." Dante peeled one of the blankets off his back and handed it to her.

"No way." She refused to take it. "I'm warm enough. You're the one who needs it."

"I'm used to this kind of cold. I grew up in the Badlands."

"I don't care where you grew up. If you drop from hypothermia, I can't carry you." She stood taller, stretching every bit of her five-foot-four-inch frame in an attempt to equal his over six-feet-tall height. "Put it back on."

He grinned, his lips as windburned as hers, and wrapped the blanket back around his shoulders. "Then let's get to it. The sooner we get there, the sooner I get my morning cup of coffee." Wrapping the blankets tightly around himself, he took off.

Emma had to hurry to keep up, shaking her head at his offer of a blanket when she had all the snow gear on and he had nothing but his underwear. Stubborn man.

Her heart warmed at his concern for her and the strength he demonstrated.

So many questions burned through her, but she saved them for when they made it to shelter and warmth. Emma focused all her energy on keeping up with the long-legged Native American marching through the snow to find help. With the sun shining brightly, the blindingly white snow made her eyes hurt and she ducked her head, her gaze on Dante's boot heels. She stepped in the tracks he left as much as possible to save energy, though his strides were far longer than hers.

After what felt like an eternity, cold to the bone, her teeth chattering so badly she couldn't hear herself think, Emma looked up and nearly cried.

A thin ribbon of smoke rose above the snow-covered landscape. Where there was smoke, there was fire and warmth. Fueled by hope, she picked up the pace, squinting at the snowy fields until the shape of a ranch house was discernible.

Less than a tenth of a mile from the house, Emma stumbled and fell into the snow. Too stiff to move quickly, she didn't get her arms up in time to keep from performing a face-plant in the icy crystals.

Before she could roll over and sit up, she was plucked from the snow and gathered in Dante's arms.

"P-put me down," she stammered, her teeth clattering so hard she was afraid she'd bite her tongue, but was too tired to care.

"Shush," he said and continued the last tenth of a mile to the front door of the house.

Her face stinging from the cold, all she could do was wrap her arms around Dante's neck and hold on while he banged on the door.

Footsteps sounded on the other side of the solid wood door and it swung open.

"Dear Lord." An older gentleman in a flannel shirt and blue jeans stood in sock feet, his mouth dropped open.

"Sir, we need help," Dante said.

"Olaf, don't just stand there, let them in and close the door. Can't let all that heat escape with the power out." An older woman hurried up behind Olaf. "Come in, come in."

Olaf's jaw snapped shut and he stepped aside, allowing Dante to carry Emma through the door.

Even before Olaf closed the door behind them, heat surrounded Emma and tears slid down her cheeks. "We made it." She buried her face against the cool blankets covering Dante's chest.

"Set her down here on the couch in front of the fire," the woman said, urging Dante forward. She waved a golden retriever out of the way and pointed to the couch she was referring to. "The storm knocked the power out last night and we've been camping out in the living room to stay warm by the fireplace. We have a generator, but we save that for emergencies."

Emma almost laughed. To most people, a power outage would constitute an emergency. The hardy folks of North Dakota had to be really down-and-out to consider power failure to be an emergency.

Dante set Emma on the sofa and immediately began pulling off her jacket.

"Let me," the woman said. She waved Dante away. "You go thaw out by the fire." As she tugged the zipper down on Emma's jacket, she introduced herself. "I'm Marge, and that's my husband, Olaf." The woman's white eyebrows furrowed. "Should I know you? You look familiar."

"I think we met last summer. My name's Emma." Emma forced a smile past her chapped lips. "Emma Jennings from the UND Paleontology Department. I was working at the dig up until yesterday."

"I thought the site had been shut down at the end of the summer," Olaf said.

Emma shrugged. "Since we've had such a mild fall I've been coming out on weekends. I'd hoped to get in one last weekend before the permafrost."

"And then the storm last night…" Marge shook her head. "You're lucky you didn't freeze to death."

"I c-can do this," Emma protested, trying to shrug out of her jacket on her own.

Marge continued to help. "Hon, your hands are like ice. It'll be a miracle if they aren't frostbitten." The woman clucked her tongue, casting a glance over her shoulder at Dante. "And him out in the cold in nothing but his underwear. What happened?"

Olaf took the blankets from Dante and gave him two warm, dry ones. "Did your truck get stuck in the snow?"

Emma's gaze shot to Dante. She didn't want to frighten these old people.

Dante took over. Holding out his hand to Olaf, he said, "I'm Dante Thunder Horse. I'm a pilot for the Customs and Border Protection unit out of Grand Forks. My helicopter was shot down several miles from here yesterday."

Olaf's eyes widened, his grip on Dante's hand tightening before he let go.

When Dante was done filling them in on what had happened, Olaf ran a hand through his scraggly gray hair and shook his head. "Don't know what's got into this world when you can't even be safe in North Dakota."

Emma laughed, more tears welling in her eyes. After their near-death experiences, she was weepier than normal. For a short time there, she had begun to wonder if they'd find shelter before they froze.

"Mind if I use your phone?" Dante asked. "I need to let the base know I'm alive."

Marge tucked a blanket around Emma. "Olaf, hand him the phone."

Olaf gave Dante a cordless phone. Dante tapped the numbers into the keypad and held the phone to his ear and frowned. "I'm not getting a dial tone."

"Sorry. I forget, without power, this one is useless." Olaf took the phone and replaced it in the powerless charger. "Let me check the one in the kitchen."

A minute later, he returned. "The phone lines are down. Must have been knocked out along with the electricity in the storm last night."

"I need to get back to Grand Forks. My people will have sent up a search and rescue unit."

"I can get you as far as Devil's Lake," Olaf said. "But

then I'll have to turn back to make sure I get home to Mamma before nightfall."

"Don't you worry about me. I can take care of myself," Marge insisted.

"We don't want to put you in danger," Emma said.

"No, we don't," Dante agreed. "If we could get as far as Devil's Lake, we can find someone heading to Grand Forks and catch a ride with them."

"I'd take you all the way to Grand Forks, but with the snow on the road and the wife here, keeping the house warm by burning firewood..."

"We wouldn't want you to leave her alone that long," Dante assured Olaf. "It'll be a long enough drive to Devil's Lake and back."

"I'll get my truck out of the barn." Olaf hurried into the hallway leading toward the back of the house. "Mamma, find the man some of my clothes. He can't go all the way to Grand Forks in his underwear." Olaf shot a grin back at them as he pulled on his heavy winter coat, hat and gloves.

Marge left them in the living room and headed the opposite direction of her husband. When she returned, she carried a pair of jeans, an older winter jacket and a flannel shirt. "These were my son's. He's a bit taller than Olaf. They should fit you better."

"I'll have them returned to you as soon as possible."

"Don't bother. He has more in the closet and he rarely makes it up here in the wintertime. We usually go stay with him and his family in January and February. They live in Florida." She grinned. "It's a lot nicer down there at this time of year than up here."

Dante smiled at the woman and accepted the clothing graciously.

"There's a bathroom in the hallway if you'd like to dress in there." Marge pointed the direction.

Dante disappeared and reappeared a few minutes later dressed in jeans that fit a little loose around his hips and were an inch or two short on his legs. The flannel shirt strained against his broad shoulders, but he didn't say a word.

Emma figured he was grateful to have anything more than just thermal underwear on his body.

He shrugged into the old jacket and zipped it. "I'll go help Olaf with the truck."

"Stay inside," Marge insisted. "You've been exposed to the weather enough for one day."

"I'm fine." He nodded toward Emma, his dark eyes smoldering. "I'll be back in a minute for you."

Emma's heart fluttered. She knew he didn't mean anything by the look, other than he'd be back to load her up in the truck.

Alone with Marge, Emma wished she was warm enough to go out and help, but the thought of going out in the cold so soon after nearly dying in it didn't appeal to her in the least. How did Dante do it?

"That's some man you have there," Marge said, fussing over the blankets in Emma's lap.

Emma started to tell Marge that he wasn't her man, but decided it didn't matter. The farmer and his wife had been very helpful, taking them in and providing them warmth and clothing.

"How long have you two been together?" Marge asked out of the blue.

Now that she hadn't refuted Marge's earlier statement, Emma didn't know whether she should tell her they weren't together. "Not very long" were the words she came up with. They were true in the simplest sense.

She and Dante had only been together since she'd found him in the snow beside the helicopter wreckage the day before and one other time when they'd had coffee together on campus.

Marge smiled. "You two make a nice couple. Now, do you want to take an extra jacket with you? Olaf keeps blankets and a sleeping bag in the backseat of the truck in case we get marooned out in bad weather. Make use of them. I know once you get cold, it's hard to warm up. Sometimes it takes me days for my old body to catch up."

Used to the North Dakota winters, Emma nodded. To think Dante was out in that cold wind helping the old man get the truck ready sent another shiver across Emma's skin.

"I've got my camp stove going and some water heating for coffee. If you're all right by yourself, I'll rustle up some breakfast for the two of you."

"You don't have to go to all that trouble." Emma's belly growled at the thought of food.

Marge laughed. "No trouble at all. We rarely have visitors so far north. It'll be a treat to get to fuss over someone." She left Emma on the couch.

The rattle of pans preceded the heavenly scent of bacon cooking. By the time the men came in from the cold, Emma's mouth was watering and she pushed aside the blankets to stand.

"Everything's ready," Dante said.

"Good. Then come have a seat at the table and eat breakfast while Olaf and I have our lunch. No use going off with an empty stomach." Marge set plates of hot food on the table and cups of steaming coffee.

"We really appreciate all you've done for us. Truthfully, we'd have been happy just to sit in front of the fire to thaw." Emma sat in the chair Dante pulled out for her and stared down at eggs, bacon, ham and biscuits. "Breakfast never looked so good," she exclaimed.

"You're an angel." Dante hugged the older woman and waited for her to sit in front of a sandwich and chips before he took his seat.

Marge's cheeks bloomed with color.

"My Marge can make most anything with a camp stove and a Dutch oven. And she can dress a mule deer like a side of beef."

Marge waved at her husband. "He only married me because I liked hunting."

Olaf grinned. "And she was the prettiest girl in the county."

Emma hid a smile. The pair clearly loved each other. "How long have you two been together?"

Olaf's head tipped to one side. "What's it been? Thirty years or more?"

Marge shook her head. "Going on forty."

"And you still don't look a day over twenty-nine."

"Big fibber."

Emma caught Dante's smile and joined him with one of her own. The warm food and good company went a long way toward restoring her stamina.

By the time Marge and Olaf bundled them into the truck, Emma was beginning to think all was right in a crazy world. She found it hard to believe that only that morning someone had tried to kill them.

As Olaf drove the long, snow-covered road to Devil's Lake, Emma had far too much time on her hands to think. Whoever had shot down Dante's helicopter hadn't been satisfied with him being injured. He'd come back to finish the job. The big question was, would he try again?

## Chapter Five

At the truck stop at Devil's Lake, Dante was able to get a call through to headquarters. The dispatcher on duty was relieved to hear from him. They'd sent out several helicopters to circle the last known location of his helicopter. The snow had done a nice job of hiding the crash site and they'd just located it beneath three feet of powder when Dante had made contact.

Dante waited while the dispatcher connected him to his supervisor, Jim Kramer.

"T.H., where the hell have you been?"

Dante laughed. "Slogging through three feet of snow to get to someplace warm."

"You had us all worried out here when you didn't show up at quittin' time."

"Nice to know someone cares." Dante had been with the CBP long enough to be a part of the team. When a chopper went down, everyone took it personally. The loss of a teammate hit everyone hard. "Rest assured, I'm not dead, yet."

"Glad to hear it." Jim paused. "What happened?"

"I was shot down by a man with a Soviet-made RPG."

"What?"

"Look, I'm sitting at a truck stop in Devil's Lake. The storm hit this area pretty hard and a lot of electric and phone lines are down. I was about to hit up a few of the truck drivers to see if anyone could get us back to Grand Forks. When I get back, I'll fill you in on all the details."

"Fair enough. But I can do you one better. Biacowski is out searching for you. I'll send him over to pick you up."

"As long as he has room for two."

"What do you mean?"

"I had a little help getting away from the burning fuselage and then surviving the storm last night by someone who works out at the university."

"Thank him for me, will ya? You know how hard it is to find good pilots."

"Will do." Dante didn't bother to correct his supervisor on the gender of the person who'd helped him. After arranging a location to pick him up, Dante hung up and turned to find Emma hugging Olaf.

Something that felt oddly like jealousy tugged at his insides. Not that he had anything to fear from Olaf. The man was married and old enough to be Emma's father.

What bothered him was that she'd felt comfortable hugging the old guy and hadn't so much as touched Dante since they'd made it back to civilization.

When Samantha was alive, he'd been jealous of any man she'd so much as said hello to. Which was practically everyone in camp. She'd laughed and told him to get over it. Though he'd never told her, he never had. His love for her had bordered on obsessive. If he was honest with himself, he was certain had Samantha lived, he'd have driven her away. She had a mind of her own and resented when he told her what to do.

He'd only done so out of fear of losing her. And his fear had played out. Samantha had died outside the wire.

Glancing across at Emma, he could see very few similarities between the two women. Where Samantha had straight, sandy-blond hair and gray-blue eyes, Emma had curly dark hair and dark brown eyes.

Being a female captain in the army meant Samantha had to have a tough exterior and confidence to command the soldiers in her company. Emma appeared to be afraid of men. But she'd shown no fear when she'd used her snowmobile to ram into the guy shooting at him. Her fear was in being alone and naked with a man.

Samantha had been hot as hell in bed and liked being on top half the time. Emma…

Her soft brown eyes met his and she smiled. Though she wasn't as sexy as Samantha, she had her own sweet serenity that made him calm and excited all at once. His heartbeat fluttered and he longed to be naked with her, buried beneath the blankets, touching her, bringing her body and senses to life.

She'd been like an exotic flower opening for the first time. And she'd given him something special, something she couldn't take back. Too bad he wasn't in the market for a relationship. Emma would be well worth the trouble.

Her cheeks grew pink.

Dante realized he must have been staring and shifted his gaze to the sky. The thumping sound of helicopter blades was music to his ears. His heart was heavy at the thought of the crashed Eurocopter AS-350 lying in a burned-out heap beneath the snow on Olaf's ranch. Helicopters weren't cheap and took time to replace. He'd gone over and over in his mind what he could have or should have done in the situation, but nothing would undo what had been done.

Biacowski set the helicopter down in a field bordering the small town of Devil's Lake.

Olaf drove the pair to the edge and let them out close enough to walk to the aircraft.

Once again, Emma hugged the older man and thanked him.

Dante stuck out his hand and shook Olaf's. "Thank you for all you and your wife have done for us."

"Thank you for your service, Dante. I hope you and your girl will come visit us again." The man grinned. "Hopefully under better circumstances next time."

Emma gave him a gentle smile. "We'd like that."

The pilot remained with the aircraft as Dante and Emma approached, hunched over to avoid being hit by the still-turning rotors. Once Dante had Emma settled in the backseat and buckled in, he handed her a headset so that she could hear the conversation up front.

Finally, Dante climbed into the copilot seat.

Dante settled the spare headset over his ears.

Biacowski glared at him. "Don't ever scare me like that again."

"Sorry to inconvenience you." Dante chuckled. "I have a feeling that if you hadn't called in sick, one or both of us would have been dead in that fire. I seriously doubt that as much as Emma helped, she could have saved both of us."

Chris glanced over his shoulder at Emma and gave her a thumbs-up. "I owe you one. Emma, is it?"

She nodded.

"Hell, the CBP owes you one. Dante's one of our best pilots."

She adjusted the mic over her mouth and spoke softly. "Glad to help."

Biacowski leaned toward Dante. "Where'd you find her? She's cute."

Dante glanced back at Emma, knowing full well she

could hear what the pilot said. "I didn't find her, she found me."

"I want the whole story when we get back."

"You got it. Just get us back before nightfall. It's already been a long day for both of us."

Dante settled back in his seat, thinking he'd close his eyes and take a short nap on the way back. A glance to the rear proved Emma had nodded off. She had to be exhausted after nearly being killed and then slogging through knee-deep snow to find shelter.

Though he closed his eyes, the rumble of the engine and the thumping of the rotors made his blood pump faster and his hands itch to take the controls. Giving up on a nap, he opened his eyes and scanned the snow-covered landscape below, half expecting to find a man on a snowmobile pointing an RPG at him.

His nerves knotted and remained stretched tight until the lights of the Grand Forks International Airport blinked up at him.

Biacowski hovered over the landing area and set the helicopter down like laying a sleeping baby in its crib.

Dante climbed into the backseat before the rotors had time to stop spinning and helped Emma out of the harness.

"I'll take you home as soon as I debrief my commander." He stared into her sleepy eyes. "Will you be okay for an hour or two?"

"I can catch a taxi back. You don't have to worry about me."

"My supervisor will want to hear your story, as well. You actually saw the man who fired on my helicopter."

"I didn't see much."

"Whatever you saw, he'll want to know about." Dante

grabbed her hand and led her toward the building. Bia-cowski followed.

Jim Kramer met them at the door to his office, showed them in and offered them coffee. "Do I need to get an ambulance to have you two taken to the hospital?" Kramer frowned, staring hard at them. "You both look like you got rolled in a fight."

Dante's gaze met Emma's and he sighed. "We did get rolled and almost lost the fight." He told his side of what had happened over the past twenty-four hours and waited while Kramer questioned Emma.

"Could you describe the man on the snowmobile?"

Emma shook her head. "Other than he had black hair, no. He was seated, so I couldn't get a feel for how tall he was and it all happened so fast, I was more worried about him running over Dante than getting a clear description of him."

Kramer came around the side of his desk and held out his hand to Emma. "Thank you for saving one of my best pilots." His lips twisted. "He's also a vital member of this team and we'd have missed him."

Dante shifted in his chair, uncomfortable with the praise when he'd allowed himself to get shot down. "Sir, whoever shot me out of the sky came back to finish the job. When he finds out he wasn't successful, he could be back. And if he thinks for a moment that Emma could identify him, he'll be after her."

Kramer leaned against his government-issued metal desk and ran his hand over his chin. "You have a point. I suppose I could assign a man to keep an eye on her."

Emma leaned forward in her chair. "I don't need anyone to keep an eye on me. I'm fully capable of taking care of myself."

Kramer shook his head. "Whoever did it has to know

it's a federal crime to shoot at a government agent. If there's any chance you can identify him, he might come after you next."

Dante leaned toward her and took her hand. "Let the boss assign an agent to you. At least until we catch the bastard."

Emma's lips pressed into a tight line, her cheeks filled with color. "No, thank you. I'm off for the next four weeks on Christmas break. I'll be vigilant and watch my back. No need to tie up resources babysitting me."

Kramer glanced at Dante. "I can't force her to accept help."

Dante's gaze met Emma's. From the stubborn look on her face he could tell she didn't like having people make decisions for her. But after all she'd done for him, he needed to be sure no one would come after her. He turned back to his boss. "I have a lot of use-or-lose vacation time on the books, right?"

"Yes, you do," Kramer confirmed.

"I'd planned on spending a little time with my family at the Thunder Horse Ranch over the holidays. If it's all right by you, I'd like to take my leave now. I'll spend part of it with Emma until we figure out who was responsible for destroying a perfectly good helicopter and then tried to kill us."

"Do I have a say in any of this?" Emma asked.

Dante's lips quirked up on the corners. "Only if it's to agree."

"Well, I won't." She pushed to a standing position. "I like my solitude and I don't need someone treating me as a charity case and guarding me as if I were a child."

Admiring her gumption, but no less determined, Dante stood beside her. "If it helps, you won't even know I'm there. I'll keep an eye on you from the comfort of my vehicle outside your apartment." He knew even before he said the words that they would get her ire up. And they did.

"Like a stalker?" She straightened.

Kramer stood, chuckling. "I'll let you two duke it out. I have a schedule to juggle. As of now, you're to report to the hospital for a quick checkup, and then you're on leave until after the first of the year. You're dismissed. And, T.H., try to stay out of the cold this time. The temperature outside is minus fifteen with a windchill of minus thirty and it's supposed to drop tonight to minus forty."

"Trust us. We don't plan on spending tonight in the elements," Dante assured his boss. "Although, it wasn't all bad."

Kramer left his office and headed down the hallway to the hangar.

When Dante turned to Emma, he noted the blush rising up Emma's neck into her cheeks.

"I won't be responsible for you missing out on family time during the holidays," she muttered.

Dante's lips twitched, but he fought the smile. She was deflecting his reference to their lovemaking and he found it endearingly cute. "I promise to spend some of my leave with my family."

"And you really don't have to spend any of it with me."

"What if I like being with you?" he quipped.

"What if I don't like being with *you?*" Twin red flags flew in her cheeks and her brown eyes flashed.

This was an Emma he liked as much as the soft, sexy one he'd made love to in the little trailer. He pulled her into an empty office and lifted both of her hands in his. "Do you really mean that?"

"You said so yourself, 'no guarantees.' Don't start feeling sorry for me."

"I don't feel sorry for you. I'm worried about you."

"Well, stop. I can take care of myself. I have for years."

"Fair enough." Rubbing his thumbs over the backs of her hands, he gazed into her eyes. "You're independent and you've taken care of yourself for a while. But have you ever had someone try to kill you before today?"

She opened her mouth to retort, but nothing came out.

"No," he answered for her. "Well, I have, and it's not fun. And it's not the right time to be on your own."

"I don't need you to be my bodyguard."

"Emma." His grip tightened on her hands. "What are you afraid of? The bad guy or me?"

She blurted out, "I'm not afraid of either." Her head dipped and she stared at her boots. "I'm afraid of me."

His heart melted at the way her bottom lip wobbled. "Why?"

Her glance shifted to the corner of the room and she didn't say anything for a full ten seconds. Then she admitted, "I've been independent for so long, I'm afraid of becoming dependent on anyone."

Dante suspected there was a lot more to her fierce independence than having been that way for a long time. Someone in her past must have hurt her. "Relying on someone else doesn't have to be a bad thing. And it's only temporary. Once we catch the bad guy, you can go back to being independent."

She didn't throw it back in his face, so he figured she was wavering. He went in for the clincher.

"Besides, you saved my life twice." He lifted one of her hands to his lips and pressed a kiss there. "I owe you. And if you don't let me pay you back by providing you a little protection in the short term, I'll always owe you my life. You can't let me go through life with such a huge obligation hanging over me, can you? It will threaten my manhood."

Her brows knitted. "You don't owe me anything. And there's nothing in this world that could possibly threaten your...er...manhood."

The way she stumbled over the last word made him think back to the trailer when her soft curves had pressed against his hard body. In an instant, he was hard all over again.

Her cheeks flamed and he could swear she was there with him.

"Please." He hooked her hand through the crook of his arm. "Let me play bodyguard for a little while. You won't regret it."

She sucked in a deep breath and let it out. "Do you really think I could be in danger? Me? I live the most boring life imaginable. How could I be a threat to anyone?"

"You saw his face."

"Surely whoever it was will assume we died in the trailer," she argued.

"When he discovers the fact that we didn't, he could come back to finish the job."

"I *barely* saw his face."

"He doesn't know that. He would only know that you and I are still alive, and we could possibly identify him."

Emma heaved another sigh. "Okay. I'll let you play bodyguard, but only for a couple of days. Surely by then they'll find out who started this whole mess."

Satisfied that he had her agreement to keep an eye on her, Dante didn't tell her that the shooter might never be found. He'd take one day at a time until his leave ran out. Maybe he was overreacting. If he did nothing and something happened to Emma, he'd never forgive himself.

THE AIRPORT WAS several miles away from the city of Grand Forks. As they stepped out into the bitter wind, Emma looked around, gathering her coat around her chin. "Are we taking a cab back to Grand Forks?"

"No." Dante guided her toward the parking lot. "I parked my Jeep out here."

A shiver shook her from the tip of her head to her toes and left her teeth chattering. "By chance does it have heated seats?"

He pulled his key fob out of his pocket and hit a button. "As a matter of fact, it does."

"Thank God," she said through chattering teeth.

"And even better, it has a remote starter and should be warming up by the time we get to it."

A dark pewter Jeep Wrangler with a hard top and raised suspension roared to life a hundred yards from where they stood.

"Yours?" Emma nodded toward the sound of the engine.

"Mine." He shrugged. "I always wanted one. I'd been saving for it since I got back from the sandbox."

Emma glanced up at him. "Sandbox?"

"Afghanistan."

She pulled her collar up around her ears to keep the wind from blowing down the back of her neck. "Were you a pilot in the war?"

He nodded, his gaze on the car ahead.

That explained his nightmare when she'd woken him in the trailer. At first she'd thought it was from having crashed in the helicopter, but it had seemed even more deep-seated. He'd said he'd been shot at before. It had to have been then.

She wondered what scars he carried from his time on

active duty. Did he have post-traumatic stress disorder? Had he watched members of his unit die?

Clouds had moved back in to cover the warming sun, and the north wind blew hard enough that Emma had to lean into it to get to the Jeep. Windchill of minus thirty was hard to take even when one wasn't tired and worn down from trudging for miles in the snow and cold. By the time they reached the Jeep, she practically fell into its warmth.

The drive into Grand Forks was conducted in silence. As Dante turned left when Emma would have turned right to go to her apartment, she remembered she hadn't given him directions. "I live in an apartment close to the university."

"And I live in an apartment on the south side of town." He shot a glance her way. "I thought we'd stop there first so that I could collect some clothes that fit and a few items I'll need."

"Need for what?"

"To stay with you."

"With me?"

"Well, yes. I thought we had this all settled. I'm your bodyguard for the next few days."

"But that doesn't mean you'll be staying with me."

"How else am I supposed to guard your body if I'm not in the same building with you?"

"But…" She bit down on her lip and stared out the window. "My apartment is really small." The thought of the hulking Native American in her apartment threatened to overwhelm her. And they weren't even in her apartment yet.

"We could stay in my apartment, but I thought you'd be more comfortable in yours."

She searched for the words she needed to set her world back to rights. Emma Jennings lived an ordered existence. Ever since a certain helicopter had crash-landed close to her dig, her life had been anything but ordered. *Chaos* was the word that best described the world she'd been thrown into.

"We'll stay in my apartment," she snapped. "But that's as far as it goes. You can sleep on the couch."

Dante sat in the driver's seat, his lips quivering on the corners.

If he smiled, she'd...she'd...ah hell, she'd probably fall all over herself and drool like a fool. The man had entirely too much charm and charisma for a lonely college professor to resist.

*I'm doomed.*

Dante glanced her way. "Did you say something?"

"Not at all," she squeaked and clamped her lips shut tight. Just because they'd made love once, didn't mean they'd hop right back into the sack at her apartment. He wasn't into commitment, and making love more than once would be too much like commitment to Emma. No, she couldn't take it if she made the mistake of falling for the handsome border patrol agent. No, he wasn't the kind of guy to stick around. The men in her life had a way of disappearing just about the time she started to think they might stick around.

It would be better to keep her distance from Dante and save herself the trouble of a broken heart.

She swallowed a groan. How the hell was she going to keep her distance when he would be camped out in her apartment?

# Chapter Six

"I'll stay here in the Jeep while you collect your belongings," Emma offered when they pulled up outside Dante's apartment building.

"Sorry." Dante tilted his head toward her. "What kind of bodyguard would I be if I left you out here in the cold, alone? Bundle up. You're coming in with me."

Emma didn't know what she expected when she entered Dante's apartment. As good as he'd been to her since she'd defended him against the shooter, she didn't know much about him. She expected his apartment to reveal something about his life. Instead, it was as stark and impersonal as a doctor's office.

Dante went to the kitchen first and grabbed a cordless phone. "I need to check in with my family in case they got word of my crash."

Dante headed for the bedroom, speaking into the telephone as he went. Apparently he got an answering machine. "Mom, it's Dante. In case you've seen the news reports about the helicopter crash involving a border patrol agent, I'm okay. Yes, it was mine, but I'm not hurt. Call me when you get a chance. Love you."

While Dante was leaving the message and packing his bag, Emma studied what little there was in the living room and kitchen.

The furniture was plain and functional with a brown leather couch and lounge chair and a rather plain coffee table and television. On the bar that separated the kitchen from the living area were two framed photos. One was of a family of six. Four brothers and their mother and father. All the men were like Dante, swarthy, black-haired and built like brick houses.

Emma peered closer. The second man from the left had to be Dante several years ago. It was him, with a few less creases around his eyes and a happy, carefree smile.

Emma found herself wishing she'd known that happier, younger Dante before he'd been jaded by a war half a world away.

"Dante, is this picture in the kitchen of your family?"

"Yes," he called out from the bedroom.

"How old is this photo? You look so much younger."

"It was taken about four years ago, when my father was still alive."

So his father was dead. Another detail of Dante's life she was learning. "I'm sorry."

"We were, too." Dresser drawers opened and closed and a closet door was opened.

Emma set the frame on the counter and lifted the other.

The other photo was of Dante in a flight suit, standing with a couple of men and one woman in desert camouflage uniforms. Dante had his arm around the woman. She wore her hair pulled back in a tight, neat bun, her makeup-free face smiling into the camera. Sandy-blond hair and light gray-blue eyes, she was a woman men could easily fall in love with. She had one of those sweet, outgoing, girl-next-door faces with an added dose of steel. She'd have to have been tough enough to handle the ten-to-one men-to-women ratio in the desert.

Emma admired women who volunteered for armed services. She herself had tried to go into ROTC, but an injury to her shoulder as a child had kept her from passing the physical.

Emma stared down at Dante's arm draped over the woman's shoulder. In her heart she knew this woman had meant something to Dante.

"What are you doing?" Dante demanded.

Emma jumped and dropped the photo frame back on the counter. She'd been so engrossed in the two photographs she hadn't noticed Dante had returned to the living area carrying a duffel bag and wearing freshly laundered jeans and a blue chambray shirt. He was even sexier in clothes that fit.

A guilty flush burned her cheeks at being caught snooping about his private life. But she refused to ignore the picture, wanting to know more about this man she'd made love to. "Who is she?"

He started to walk by, headed for the door, but stopped beside her instead. "Someone I used to know."

Lifting the frame again, she stared across the floor at him. "She's very pretty."

Dante's gaze went to the photo, his eyes staring as if looking back in time, not at the paper picture but at the memories it inspired. "Samantha made the desert bearable."

Something in his voice made Emma's heart squeeze in her chest, but she couldn't stop herself from observing, "She has a nice smile."

He nodded. "Everyone at Bagram Airfield loved Samantha."

Emma studied Dante's face, her heart settling into the pit of her belly. "Did you love her?"

His gaze shifted from the photo to Emma. "What?"

"Did you love her?"

"Yes."

"And do you still?" Emma asked quietly.

His lips thinned, his dark green eyes unreadable. "Yes."

Emma glanced around the sterile apartment. There were no signs of the woman. Surely he wouldn't have taken Emma out to have coffee if he was still involved with her. "What happened?" she dared to ask, the question burning in her heart.

"She died in an IED explosion while visiting an Afghan orphanage outside the wire."

A heavy lump settled in the pit of Emma's gut as she stared down at the beautiful face, so happy and alive. "That's terrible."

"Yeah," he said, the word clipped and as emotionless as the room they stood in. "Ready?"

Emma nodded and set the frame on the counter. "I'm sorry for your loss. She must have been a very special woman."

"She was."

And there she had it. Samantha was a very special woman. How could Emma compete with that? No wonder he'd had coffee with her one time and walked away without calling again. Emma didn't measure up to Samantha's perfection.

Her heart fell even farther, landing somewhere around her shoes. And he'd made love to her only to find out she was a pathetic virgin. Heat burned her cheeks and she ducked her head to hide her shame. "I'm ready to leave."

She led the way through the door and stopped on the threshold. "I really wish you'd just drop me off and forget about this bodyguard gig."

Dante frowned. "Why are we arguing about it again?

I thought we'd settled this. I'm going to stay with you for a few days. I promise not to get in your way."

How could he not get in her way? Dante Thunder Horse was larger than life and had given his heart to a dead woman.

Emma had to remind herself that Dante wasn't providing her protection to get closer to her. Why should he? He'd had perfection. Making love to Emma had probably been just something that had happened to keep them warm.

Pushing all thoughts of sex with Dante to the back of her mind, Emma squared her shoulders and nodded. "You're right. It's only for a few days. Then you'll be on your way home to your family and I'll go back to my work as a professor." Spending Christmas by herself as usual. How pathetic was that?

Because her mother had died and she hadn't spoken to her father since, she had no one. Christmas was one of those holidays she dreaded each year. This year would be no different.

Dante threw his duffel bag into the back of his Jeep and opened the door for Emma. She slid past him, careful not to touch him and set off all those errant nerve endings that jumped anytime he was near. He might not see her as a potential sexual partner, but Emma's body sure couldn't forget her first time making love. The man had been amazing. Her foot slipped as she stepped up on the Jeep's running board and she crashed back into Dante.

His arms surrounded her and he crushed her to his chest.

Emma's heart thundered against her ribs. His arm crossed her chest beneath her breasts, one of his big hands covering her tummy. Even through her thick winter coat, she could feel his warmth.

In that instant, in his arm, her thoughts scrambled. For a moment, she imagined him holding her because he wanted to, not because she'd practically thrown herself at him. Accidentally, of course.

Once she had her feet under her, she tried to push out of his arms.

"Steady there," he said. "That running board can get slick in the icy weather."

*Now he tells her.* "I'm okay. I'll be more careful next time."

"Oh, I didn't mind. I just want to make sure you're not hurt."

"Thanks." As she scrambled into the Jeep, she felt his palm on her rear, making certain she didn't fall back this time.

Embarrassed by her clumsiness and her body's instant reaction, she settled into the leather seat and turned her face away from Dante as he climbed into the driver's seat. She gave him the directions to her apartment and sat in silence as he drove across town.

She tried not to look his way, but she couldn't help it. The man had the rugged profile of his ancestors, complete with chiseled cheekbones and a strong jaw.

Several times he glanced into the rearview mirror, his brows furrowing.

"What's wrong?" Emma finally asked as they approached the street to her apartment complex. When they passed her turn, she swiveled in her seat. "You missed my turn."

"I can't swear to it, but I think someone was following us."

Emma spun to look behind her. "In Grand Forks?"

"I know it's a small city by most standards, and there aren't that many places for people to go, but the vehicle

behind me has been on my tail since I left my apartment."
Dante relaxed. "Good, he turned off." Dante sped up and
turned at the next corner, going the long way around to
circle back to her apartment complex.

"It could be my imagination, but I'd rather be safe
than sorry." He pulled into the parking lot and parked
the Jeep on the far side of a trash bin, out of visible range
of the street.

Emma thought he was taking his job as a bodyguard
to the extreme, but didn't say anything. This was Grand
Forks, North Dakota, not Chicago or Houston.

As soon as he put the Jeep in Park, Emma unbuckled
her belt and carefully climbed out to stand on the ground.
She didn't want a repeat performance of her earlier awkward actions.

"I'm on the second floor." She led the way up the outside staircase to the entrance of her apartment and bent
to retrieve her spare key from beneath a flowerpot with
a dead plant covered in a dusting of snow.

"You really shouldn't leave a key to your apartment
out here. Anyone could get in."

"I've been living by myself for years."

"I know, but still, it's not safe."

"Well, since my purse is in my crashed truck at the
dig site, I'm glad I had a key beneath the flowerpot. It's
almost impossible to catch the apartment manager in his
office on a weekend." She unlocked the door and entered,
switching on the lights.

Nothing in her apartment had changed. After all that
had happened, it seemed both anticlimactic and reas-
suring at the same time. "You can set your bag by the
couch," she said. "I'm sorry, but I don't have a lot of
groceries. I had planned on stocking up when I got back
from the dig site."

"We can go to the store when you want."

"I need to call my insurance agent and deal with my truck and I guess the state police to report the accident." She turned toward him shaking her head. "I'm not even sure what I'm supposed to do."

"I'll take you down to the state police station and we can give a statement. My supervisor should already have given them a heads-up. That should get the ball rolling. They might want to bring in the Feds since it was attempted murder and an attack on federal property."

"And a federal agent," Emma reminded him. He seemed more concerned about the helicopter than his own life.

He shrugged and continued. "The National Transportation Safety Board will investigate the downed helicopter. And the Department of Homeland Security will also want to get involved as it could be considered a terrorist attack since the man used a Soviet-made RPG to shoot me down."

A tremor shook Emma. "We're in North Dakota, not Afghanistan."

Dante's face grew grim. "And the attacks on the Twin Towers and the Pentagon were here in America."

"It's hard to accept that nowhere can be considered safe anymore."

A vehicle alarm system went off in the parking lot below her apartment, making Emma jump. She laughed shakily. "Guess I'm getting punchy."

Dante strode to the window, glanced out through the blinds and shook his head. "That's my Jeep. I guess someone bumped into it accidentally. The alarm is supersensitive."

Emma joined him at the window and stared down at his SUV. The lights blinked and a siren wailed.

Digging his key fob from his jeans pocket, Dante aimed it at the vehicle. The alarm and blinking lights ceased and it grew quiet again.

Emma hadn't realized just how close she was standing next to Dante until she turned to face him at the same time as he faced her.

"Better?" he asked with a smile.

She nodded, her tongue suddenly tied, words beyond her as she stared at those lips that had kissed her senseless.

He reached out to cup her cheek. "I promise I'll do my best to protect you." Then ever so gently, he brushed his mouth across hers.

Emma exhaled on a sigh, her body leaning into his as if drawn to him of its own accord.

He slipped a hand around to the small of her back, and the one cupping her cheek rounded to the back of her neck, urging her forward as he returned for a longer, deeper kiss.

His tongue thrust between her teeth, sliding along hers in a sensuous caress that left her breathless.

The hand at her back slipped beneath her sweater, fingers splaying across her naked skin.

She wished she was completely naked, lying beside his equally naked body. Though she was unskilled in the art of making love, she'd follow his lead and they'd—

A car door slammed outside, breaking through her reverie.

Dante lifted his head and glanced out the window. "I'm sorry. I promised you wouldn't even know I was here. That kiss was uncalled for."

"That's okay." She wanted to tell him that she'd liked it, but didn't want to sound too naive or desperate. Though every ounce of her being wanted him to pull her back into his arms and kiss her again.

Dante's hands fell to his sides and he stuffed them into his pockets.

Emma couldn't move away, afraid her wobbly knees wouldn't hold her up. Instead, her gaze followed his to the parking lot below where backup lights blinked bright and a truck eased out of the parking space beside Dante's SUV.

Emma tensed. The driver was turning too sharp and his tires didn't seem to be getting enough traction to straighten the vehicle.

"He's going to hit your Jeep," Emma said, diving for the door. She flung it open and started to shout to the driver to stop.

Before she could get a word out, the world seemed to explode in front of her.

EMMA WAS BLOWN backward, hitting Dante square in the chest, knocking him onto the floor of her apartment. He fell flat on his back and Emma landed on top of him. With the wind knocked out of him and his ears ringing, he lay for a moment trying to comprehend what had just happened.

Then he was scrambling to his feet and racing down the steps to the parking lot below. His Jeep was a black-ened hulk with a hole blown through the driver's side.

The truck that had been backing out of the space next to his was drifting backward across the icy surface of the pavement, the hood had been blown upright and the driver was slumped at the wheel. Smoke billowed out of the engine.

Dante ran to the truck and yanked at the door. It was locked. He banged on the window and shouted to get the driver's attention, but he wasn't waking up no matter how hard Dante banged or how loud he shouted.

The truck slid back into a car and stopped, but smoke billowed from the engine compartment and then flames sprang from the source of the smoke.

Desperate to get the man out of the truck, he glanced around for something to break the window with. The ground and the sidewalks were covered in snow from the night before and nothing jumped out that would be strong enough to break the glass.

Behind him, he heard footsteps clambering down the stairs and Emma slid to a stop beside him. "Use this," she said and slapped a hammer in his palm.

Dante gave a brief grin. Emma was smart and resourceful.

He rounded to the passenger side of the vehicle and slammed the hammer into the glass. It took several attempts before he broke all the way through and could reach his hand in to hit the automatic door-lock release.

As soon as he did, Emma pulled open the driver's door and reached inside to unbuckle the seat belt.

The flame surged, the heat making Dante's face burn. "Get back!" he shouted, racing around the other side of the truck.

Emma ignored his entreaty and tugged at the driver's arm. "We have to get him out."

Dante arrived at her side. As soon as she backed away, he grabbed the man and pulled him out, draping his limp body over his shoulder. He turned and nearly ran into Emma. "Move, move, move!"

With the burden of the man weighing him down and the ice-covered pavement slowing his steps, Dante ran after Emma, barely making it to the apartment building before the flame found the truck's gas tank. The second explosion in less than ten minutes rocked the earth beneath them and he crashed to his knees on the concrete.

Emma appeared in front of him and soon other apartment dwellers emerged from their rooms to see what all the commotion was.

Emma pointed to a woman who stood in the doorway of her apartment with her hair up in a towel and yelled, "Lisa, call 9-1-1!"

The woman's eyes widened and she spun back into her apartment and reappeared with her cell phone pressed to her ear, talking rapidly to the dispatcher on the other end.

"Here, lean on me. Let me help you up." Emma slipped one of Dante's arms over her shoulder and helped him to rise with the man in tow. Grateful for her help, he tried not to put too much weight on her as he clambered to his feet.

"We should get him inside where it's warm," Emma said, angling toward the woman on the cell phone.

She stepped back and let them enter.

Dante laid the man out on the couch and straightened.

"I need blankets," Emma said.

Lisa, still holding the phone, nodded toward the hallway. "The ambulance and fire department are on their way. The dispatcher wants me to stay on the phone until they arrive. You can find blankets in the hall closet."

"I'll get them." Emma disappeared and reappeared with two thick blankets.

Sirens wailed and soon the apartment building was surrounded by emergency vehicles, lights flashing. Firemen leaped out and quickly extinguished the blaze, but not before two other cars had sustained damage.

The emergency medical technicians brought in a backboard and loaded the driver onto it and carried him out to the ambulance.

By the time city police and the state police took their statements and the tow truck came to collect the disabled vehicles, day had turned to night. Not that the days were very long during the North Dakota winters.

Emma thanked Lisa for all her help and led the way back up to her apartment.

Dante followed her in, closed the door behind him and leaned against it.

She faced him with shadows beneath her eyes and a worried frown creasing her forehead. "If you had been in your Jeep..."

"I'd be dead. And if you'd been with me in the passenger seat, you'd be either dead or severely injured. I hope that truck driver makes it."

"Toby," she said. "His name is Toby and he's a student at UND. I hope he makes it, too. He has a promising future as an aerospace engineer." Emma ran a hand through her hair and stared across at him, her eyes glassy with unshed tears.

Dante's heart squeezed at the desperation in her tone. He opened his arms and she fell into them. Wrapping her in his embrace, he leaned his cheek against the side of her head. "It's not safe here."

"If it's not safe here, it won't be any safer at your apartment." She looked up at him with those anxious brown eyes. "We have nowhere else to go."

Dante shook his head. "Yes, we do." He turned her around and gave her backside a gentle slap. "Pack your bags. We're going to the Thunder Horse Ranch. We'll leave first thing in the morning."

# Chapter Seven

Emma lay in her bed with the goose down comforter pulled up to her chin and stared at the ceiling. Exhaustion should have knocked her right out, but for the life of her, she couldn't go to sleep. Too many thoughts tumbled in her mind, too many images of the past twenty-four hours kept replaying through her head like a recurring nightmare.

The only thing that kept her from having a full-blown anxiety attack was the man lying on the couch in her living room. Dante was the one island in the murky river of her thoughts keeping her afloat.

As independent as she thought she was, she'd give anything for him to lie beside her, take her into his arms and tell her everything was going to be all right.

She'd lean her face against his naked chest and breathe in the scent of him and all would be well with her world and she'd finally be able to go to sleep.

Like hell. If he was lying naked beside her, she'd be too tempted to run her hands over his body and explore all those interesting places she'd missed when they'd made love in the cold interior of her now-destroyed camp trailer.

Achingly aware of the man in the other room and too

wound up to lay still a moment longer, Emma finally gave in, flung back the covers and sat up.

A large shadow moved and Dante appeared in the doorway. "Can't sleep, either?" He leaned against the door frame, his arms crossed and his legs crossed at the ankles.

Emma couldn't see his expression, but the faint glow through the blinds from the security light outside her living room window backlit the man, making him appear larger than life and incredibly sexy. He wore nothing but gym shorts, his swarthy, Native American skin even darker in the dim lighting.

She swallowed hard. "No. I keep thinking back over everything that's happened."

"Me, too." He crossed the room to sit on the edge of her bed. "As soon as I lay my head down, my thoughts spin."

"You could have died. Four times."

"And you could have died almost as many."

Emma harrumphed. "I feel like a big wimp." She smiled, though her lips trembled.

"Do you mind?" He moved to sit beside her and pulled her into the crook of his arm.

Emma leaned into his body, feeling immediately warmer and more secure than before he showed up in her doorway.

"As I see it, you're pretty darned brave." He held up a thumb. "First, you risked your life by nearly crashing your snowmobile into the man who shot me down. A wimp wouldn't have done that."

Emma didn't think it had been at all heroic. "I didn't think. I just reacted."

"But you reacted. Most people would have hesitated. It took someone with a backbone to charge in...without thinking." He unfolded his pointer finger. "Second, you kept your head when the trailer was caving in around us and got the hell through the window fast enough so that I could get out. Then you helped me squeeze through. I doubt very seriously I would have made it out in time without your help."

"You would have," she insisted.

He unfolded another finger. "You walked several miles in frigid cold without a single complaint, when I know you had to be hurting."

She snorted. "And fell on my face before we made it to the house."

"And gave me an opportunity to be a hero. Carrying you that last little bit was nothing, and it made me look good to Olaf and Marge." He chuckled, the vibrations sending tiny electric shocks through her.

She turned her cheek into his bare chest and closed her eyes. Daring to touch him, she laid her hand on him and felt the rise and fall of each breath he took. "Keep talking. I'm still not convinced."

Another finger unfolded as he scooted down in the bed until he was lying beside her. "When the truck was on fire and an explosion was imminent, you risked your life to help get Toby out." His arm tightened around her. "Sweetheart, you're not a wimp. You're pretty impressive if you ask me."

She wanted to ask if she was anywhere near as impressive as Samantha, but knew it wouldn't be appropriate to compare herself to a dead woman. Dragging her into the conversation would only bring Dante more pain.

Instead, she settled against his side.

"Go to sleep, Emma. If you'd like, I'll stay awake to be on the lookout until morning."

"No, we have a long trip ahead of us and I'll bet you plan on doing most of the driving."

"I'm used to long stretches of sleeplessness. I can handle it."

"You might be able to, but I can't. Surely we'll be okay if we both get some sleep. I'm a light sleeper. I'll let you know if I hear anything strange."

"I suppose it will be all right. Do you want me to go back to the couch?"

"No," she said, her hand flexing against his chest as if that alone would keep him from getting up if he wanted to. "I promise not to seduce you."

He chuckled. "Okay, but I wouldn't be opposed if you did."

Though she wanted to feel gloriously satiated like she had felt in the trailer, she also didn't want him to think she was needy. For a moment she considered making the first move, but then squelched the idea.

Dante sighed and rolled her onto her side away from him, then spooned her body with his. "Sleep. It's been a long day and tomorrow promises to be equally trying."

"Let's hope not. I could do with less drama."

"You and me both." His arm tightened around her middle and he drew her close.

For a long time, Emma lay in Dante's arms, sleep eluding her. When his breathing became more regular and deeper, she relaxed, a little disappointed that he hadn't tried anything.

Exhaustion finally claimed her and she fell asleep, cocooned in the warmth of Dante's body, her last thought being that she could get used to this far too easily.

DANTE SLIPPED BACK into another nightmare when his helicopter had been attacked in Afghanistan.

*Having taken hits, he was barely able to bring his helicopter back to Bagram. But he had and set it down as smoothly as if it wasn't damaged. He was congratulating himself when one of the guys in the back said, "Giddings was hit. We need an ambulance ASAP."*

*As he ripped his harness loose, he gave instructions to the tower, slipped from the pilot's seat and dropped to the ground. He ran around to the other side where the gunner was being unbuckled from his harness and carried out of the craft.*

*Giddings had volunteered to be a gunner and had competed with others to claim the position. He'd been a damned good gunner, saving their butts on more than one occasion.*

*At twenty-three, he was barely out of his teens, a kid. And he had a young, pregnant wife back in the United States due to give birth in less than a month. Four weeks from redeployment back to the United States, he'd insisted on flying this mission.*

*Dante could kick himself for letting the kid fly. The closer they came to redeployment the more superstitious they became. It seemed that only the really good guys managed to be jinxed their last month in the sandbox.*

*When the ambulance arrived, Dante insisted on riding with them to the hospital and he stayed until Giddings was out of surgery and out of danger. He'd make it.*

*It had all happened so fast. One minute they were flying a mission, the next he was waiting for the doc to tell him the verdict on one of his crew.*

*It wasn't until he was on his way back to his quarters that he made the turn to swing by Samantha's room. She would be off duty by now and he really needed to see her.*

*She shared quarters with another personnel officer, Lieutenant Mandy Brashear. He might not get her alone, but at least he could share a hug and a kiss. After nearly losing a member of his team, he really needed the reassurance of her warm body next to his.*

*When he stopped outside her door, he heard the sound of someone sobbing. Without hesitating, he pushed open the door and entered. "Samantha?"*

*Lieutenant Brashear lifted her head from her pillow and stared up at him with tear-streaked cheeks, her eyes rounding as she recognized him. "Oh, Dante," she said, ignoring the protocol of addressing a higher-ranking officer by his rank and last name. "You haven't heard?"*

*Dante stiffened, his heart seizing in his chest, guessing what Mandy would say before she did. "What's wrong? Where's Sam?" He looked around the small room, although he knew she wasn't there.*

*"Oh, God." Mandy's tears gushed from her eyes and her words became almost incoherent as she sobbed and spoke simultaneously. "She went to the orphanage today... I...can't...believe...Oh, God." She buried her face in her hands and sobbed some more.*

*His hands and heart going cold, Dante gripped Lieutenant Brashear's shoulders and lifted her to her feet. "Where is Sam?"*

*"She was in the hospital when I left her," she blurted. "Dante, she's...she's...dead."*

*Dante ran all the way back to the hospital where he'd been just minutes before, outside the surgical units, waiting for Giddings to be sewn up and released. He hadn't known that in the unit beside Giddings, Samantha had taken her last breath.*

*He got back in time to see them zip her into the body bag. They wheeled her out on a gurney. All sealed up and final. He didn't even get to say goodbye.*

"Dante," a female voice called to him.

For a moment he thought it was Samantha, but she had a gravelly voice; this was a smooth, sexy voice calling his name.

"Dante, wake up." A hand shook his shoulder this time.

Dante opened his eyes and looked up into Emma's face and blinked, for a split second wondering what she was doing in Afghanistan. Then he remembered he wasn't in the Middle East, but back in North Dakota having been attacked on multiple occasions. He rolled off the side of the bed and landed on his feet. "What's wrong?"

Emma smiled. "I'm sorry, but your cell phone is ringing. That's the third time it's rung in the past fifteen minutes."

Shaking the cobwebs from his head, he hurried into the living room and grabbed his cell phone off the coffee table where he'd left it. In the display window was the word Mom.

It was two o'clock in the morning. She wouldn't call at this hour unless it was an emergency. These thoughts whisked through his mind as he hit the talk button. "Mom, what's wrong?"

"Oh, thank goodness you answered." She took a deep breath and let it out before continuing. "Pierce and Tuck were in an accident and are in the hospital in Bismarck."

His hand tightened on the phone. The last time he'd been at the hospital in Bismarck, his father had died from injuries sustained when he'd been thrown by his horse. "What happened?"

"Yesterday, they were on their way home for the weekend when Pierce's brakes gave out. From what the police said, they had been traveling pretty fast with the roads being clear still. This was before the big storm." His mother spoke to someone in the background and returned to the story. "They had come up on an accident on the interstate. That's when the brakes must have failed. Rather than slam into the vehicles stopped on the interstate, they drove off into the ditch. The truck flipped, rolled and landed upside down." Her voice broke on a sob.

Dante's heart squeezed hard. He wished he was there to comfort his mother. The woman was a rock and if she was in this much distress, it had to be bad.

She sniffed. "I'm sorry. I can't do this." The phone clattered as if it had been dropped.

"Mom?" Dante listened and could hear female voices. "Mom!"

"Dante, this is Julia." Julia was Tuck's wife and the mother of his little girl, Lily. "Tuck was thrown twenty yards and suffered a concussion, but Pierce was trapped inside the truck until the fire department could get there from Bismarck and cut him out. They didn't get him out until the storm hit. They almost didn't make it back to Bismarck in the ambulances."

"Damn." Though he'd been away fighting in the war and then living on the opposite end of the state of North Dakota, he was still very much a part of the Thunder Horse family and he loved his brothers. To be that close to having lost one hit him hard.

"Tuck's okay," Julia continued. "It's Pierce we're all worried about. When the truck flipped he sustained a couple of broken ribs, a punctured lung and we don't know what else. He's had some internal bleeding and he's still unconscious. They've sedated him into a medically induced coma until they can figure out what else is damaged."

Dante pinched the bridge of his nose, his own crash pushed to the back of his mind. Apparently his mother hadn't heard about it and hadn't received the message on her answering machine at the ranch. He'd have to contact the ranch foreman, Sean McKendrick, and have him erase it before she got home. No use worrying her more when he was fine.

"How's Mom holding up?"

"She's doing okay, but the emotional strain is wearing on her," Julia said. "We knew you'd planned to be here next week, but with Pierce and Tuck both in the hospital and Maddox on the other side of the world in Trejikistan with Katya and not due back until next week, we thought you might want to be here."

Dante straightened. "I'm coming home."

"Thank goodness." Julia's words came out in a rush. "Roxanne is here with Pierce, and with your mother here, the foremen of the two ranches are on their own. And, Dante…" Julia's voice dropped and she paused. Footsteps sounded at her end as if she was walking down a hallway. Then she continued, "There have been some suspicious accidents happening out there. Your mother thinks it's just bad luck, but Roxanne and I think someone is sabotaging things. We're afraid if we don't have a Thunder Horse out there keeping an eye on things, there won't be a ranch to come home to. Amelia has gone so far as to hire a security firm to set up surveillance cameras."

"Why didn't she tell me?"

"She knows she can't ask you guys to come home every time something goes bump in the night. With Maddox out of the country, she wanted something to make her feel safe. Thus the security system."

The thought of his mother being scared enough to hire a security firm bothered Dante more than he could believe. "I'll stop in at the hospital on my way through. It'll take me between four and five hours to get there. I can be there around seven in the morning."

"Oh, Dante," Julia begged, "please wait until morning. The last thing we need right now is another Thunder Horse in a ditch. And I don't think your mother could worry about one more thing."

"Okay. I'll wait until closer to sunup. Expect me at noon."

"Good. Just a minute. Your mother wanted to talk to you one more time."

Dante braced himself, his eyes burning as his mother got on the phone. "Dante, your brothers are going to be okay."

"I know, Mom. I'm worried about you."

She snorted, the sound hitching with what he suspected was a sob. "I'm a tough old bird. Don't you go worrying about me. And don't you come rushing out here thinking we all need saving. Maddox will be home before you know it, and Pierce and Tuck will be up and giving him hell. Take care of yourself, son."

"I will. I love you, Mom."

"I love you, too."

When he rang off, Dante stood for a long time, with the phone in his hand, his thoughts flipping through all the chapters in his life, so many of them, including the days he'd spent riding across the Badlands on wild ponies he and his brothers had tamed. Their Lakota blood had run strong through their veins and their mother had encouraged them to embrace their father's heritage.

*Wakantanka,* the Great Spirit, had watched over their antics, protecting them from harm.

Dante closed his eyes and lifted his face to the sky. Where was the Great Spirit when his brothers' truck had flipped? Perhaps he'd been there. Otherwise they would both be dead.

A hand on his arm brought him back to the apartment.

"What's wrong?" Emma stood beside him in a short baby-blue filmy nightgown, her pale skin practically glowing in the darkness.

"My brothers were in an accident."

She gasped. "Are they okay?"

"So far."

"You have to go to them."

"We'll leave in the morning and stop at the hospital in Bismarck on our way to the Thunder Horse Ranch."

"I meant to ask, just where is the Thunder Horse Ranch?"

"In the Badlands north of Medora."

"Okay." She smiled. "I'll be sure to pack my snow gear. In the meantime, you need sleep. It's a long way there."

He shook his head. "I can't sleep."

"Then come lay down with me. Even if you don't sleep, you can rest." She took his hand and led him back into her bedroom, offering him comfort he gladly accepted.

When he stretched out on the bed beside her, she lay in the crook of his arm, her cheek pressed to his chest, her hand draped across his belly. He lay staring at the ceiling, thinking about his brothers and his mother and wishing his father was still alive.

"Stop thinking," Emma whispered against his skin. Her warm breath stirred him, reminding him that he wasn't alone with his thoughts.

Emma skimmed her hand over his chest and down his torso and back up in soothing circles. "Think of something else," she urged as her hand drifted lower.

He captured her wrist before she bumped into the rising tent of his shorts. "Once again, don't go there unless you mean it."

She tipped her chin and stared up at him. The little bit of light shining around the edges of the blinds gave her face a light blue glow and her eyes shone in the darkness. "I mean it."

He let go of her wrist and her hand slid lower until it skimmed across his shaft, which became instantly hard and pulsing.

He drew in a slow steadying breath. "Why are you doing this?" A sudden thought reared its ugly head and he flipped her over on her back and pinned her wrists to the mattress.

Her eyes rounded and shone white in the darkness.

"Are you doing this out of some misguided sense of pity?"

Emma shook her head. "No. Not at all."

"Then why?"

"I'm sorry. I shouldn't have been so forward." Her eyelids swept low over her eyes. "I understand if you're not interested in someone so…so…"

"So what?" he asked.

"Inexperienced," she finished, a frown settling between delicate brows.

He nudged her knees apart and settled lower between her legs, letting the hard ridge of his erection brush up against the juncture of her thighs. "Oh, I'm interested all right. But why are you? I don't need anyone's pity."

She glanced away from him and he'd bet her cheeks were flaming. "I was curious," she whispered.

"About what?"

"If the second time would be as good as the first?" She stared up at him, the limited lighting making her face glow a dusky-blue.

The tension leached out of him and he dropped low to steal a kiss. Though it wasn't stealing when she gave it freely. Emma tasted of mint and smelled like roses, the scent light and fragrant but not overpowering. Samantha had reminded him of honeysuckle growing wild and untamed. The two women were as different as night and day.

Where Sam had captured his interest with her unfettered ability to grasp life by the horns and ride, Emma was like an English rosebud, waiting for the sunlight to unfurl.

He released her hands and bent to claim her lips in a crushing kiss. Partly because of the burning desire ignited inside him and partly out of anger for making him think about Sam again. He'd tried so hard to put that chapter of his life behind him, to forget what he'd lost in her and how life had stretched before him empty without her in it.

Quiet, studious Emma had been the first woman he'd even considered dating since Samantha's death. And after having coffee with her, he'd refused to see her again, afraid that being with her meant he was dishonoring the memory of Samantha. Or that he was finally starting to forget her.

The truth was that Samantha was gone forever and Emma was lying beneath him, willing to slake the hunger in his body. If he made love to her, it would mean nothing but a physical release to him. His body recognized needs his mind had refused to let him satisfy.

Once he started, he couldn't seem to stop and Emma didn't cry out or tell him no. Part of him wished she would.

He trailed kisses from her mouth to the edge of her jaw and down the long line of her throat to the pulse beating wildly at the base.

Her fingers curled around the back of his neck and

urged him to continue his downward path to the swells of her breasts beneath the sheer fabric of her nightgown.

He grabbed the hem and ripped it up over her head and tossed it aside.

She lay beneath him, bathed in the soft, gray-blue light shining around the edges of the blinds, her breasts peaked, the nipples tight little buds.

Dante swooped down to taste first one, then the other, rolling the taut buttons between his teeth and across his tongue. When he sucked it into his mouth, she arched her back off the bed, pressing it deeper into his mouth. He gladly accepted, flicking the tip with his tongue.

Slowly, he teased his way across her ribs, slid a hand between her legs, and parted her folds to stroke the strip of flesh hiding there.

Her breath caught and held.

When he started to remove his hand, she covered it with hers and pressed it down, encouraging him to continue.

For someone who'd never had a lover, she learned quickly and wasn't too shy to let him know what she liked.

Before long, her breathing grew ragged and she dug her heels into the mattress, her bottom rising above the sheets as she called out his name. "Dante!"

Her body pulsed beneath his fingers until finally the tension subsided and she fell back to the bed, with a shuddering sigh. "Amazing."

Dante cupped her sex and leaned up to kiss her full on the lips before lying on the bed beside her.

"Wait." Emma leaned up on her elbow, her hand going to the hard line of his manhood. "What about you?"

"Watching you was enough for me."

She frowned, her fingers curling around him. "But you're still…"

"Hard?" He laughed though it took a lot for him to force it out. "I could drive nails with it right now."

"Then, please." She tugged on him, but he refused to budge.

"I don't have protection."

"We didn't have it last night."

"And that was pushing the limits. I won't risk it again. Now, if you happen to have something…?" His lips twisted. "I thought not." He tucked an arm behind his head and pulled her up against him. "I'll take a rain check in the meantime. Sleep, Emma. I have a feeling tomorrow will be another long day."

Emma settled beside him, curled against his side. Whether he wanted her there or not, she wasn't too proud to take advantage of his offer to hold her until she went to sleep.

Warm, safe and satisfied, she drifted to sleep with a smile on her face. She had to remind herself she was an independent college professor and that when all this was over, Dante would move on and possibly never see her again.

But while she had the chance, she'd take whatever scraps he was willing to throw her way. If it meant she was desperate and lonely…well, then it was true. She *was* desperate and lonely, and whatever memories she stored up during her time with Dante would have to do.

In her life history, she was destined to be alone. The men who'd come and gone in her life had been prone to have an aversion to commitment. Emma had long since convinced herself it was her or at least the magnet she seemed to carry around that attracted men who refused to commit.

Tomorrow was another day and she'd better get some sleep if she wanted to be awake when they finally made it to the Thunder Horse Ranch.

## Chapter Eight

Dante glanced across at Emma as she leaned back in the seat of the SUV he had rented for the next couple of weeks. She hadn't spoken much throughout the trip and the circles beneath her eyes were more pronounced. Though she'd slept part of the night, they hadn't really had a decent night's sleep in two days.

The back of Dante's neck was stiff and he could feel some of the bruises and sore muscles he'd acquired in the helicopter and trailer crashes.

He'd insisted on a four-wheel-drive SUV for the trip, knowing the roads to the ranch could be difficult during the summer and impassible in a two-wheel-drive vehicle during the harsh North Dakota winters.

The insurance company would take their time sorting out the details of replacing the Jeep. A full investigation would have to be performed by the National Transportation Safety Board on the helicopter crash and the FBI would assist the state police with the case since it involved federal equipment and personnel.

If Pierce and Tuck were in any shape to assist, theirs was the closest FBI regional office to the crash site. Though they would not be assigned the case, Dante knew they would be involved enough to keep him informed of the progress.

So far, not a single terrorist organization or survivalist group had stepped forward to claim responsibility for shooting down his helicopter.

He'd checked in with his boss, who informed him that the police and investigation team from the state crime lab had combed over the burned out hull of the helicopter finding no more evidence or gleaning any more information than he'd already imparted. The snowstorm had covered the snowmobile tracks and more snow was predicted within the next twenty-four hours.

The winter that had held off until now had set in and wouldn't loosen its hold until late April.

Emma slept for the first hour and a half of the drive to Bismarck. The road crews had worked hard to clear the interstate highways between Grand Forks and Fargo and between Fargo and Bismarck. Other than a few slick spots, they hadn't had to slow too much, but the wind blowing in from the northwest pounded the rental, forcing them to use a lot more gasoline than if it had been calm.

By the time Dante reached the hospital in Bismarck, he was ready for the break before the additional three-hour trip to Thunder Horse Ranch. The clouds were settling in, making the sky a dark gray. If they didn't get on the road soon, they might not make it to the ranch. The weather reports on the radio were predicting whiteout conditions starting after dark.

As he pulled into the hospital parking lot, he braced himself for what he'd find. Cell phone reception had been limited between Fargo and Bismarck, with long stretches without any reception whatsoever.

When they'd neared Bismarck, he'd checked his phone. No missed calls and no text messages. He prayed that no news was good news, and climbed out of the car, stretching stiff muscles.

Before he could get around to the passenger side, Emma was already on the snowy ground, pulling the collar of her coat up around her ears.

They entered the hospital together. Emma took his hand and squeezed it. "If your brothers are anything like you, they'll be fine. Thunder Horse men seem to be pretty tough."

He returned the pressure on her hand, thankful she'd come with him. Dante remembered where the ICU was located having been there when his father was taken there. He'd died in the ICU shortly after he'd been admitted to the hospital.

The acrid scent of disinfectants and rubbing alcohol still brought back bad memories and reminded him of his loss.

It was exactly noon when he stepped out of the elevator and saw his mother, surrounded by Julia and Roxanne, talking to a man in a white lab coat.

Dante hurried forward, still holding on to Emma's hand. "What's going on? How's Pierce?" he demanded.

His mother turned, her face lighting up when she saw him. "Dante." She wrapped him in her arms and hugged him so tight he could barely breathe. And it felt good. Like coming home.

After a moment, he set her away from him and asked again, "How's Pierce?"

"Oh, Dante." His mother wiped a tear from the corner of her eye and Dante's stomach fell.

Roxanne stepped forward and draped an arm around Amelia's shoulders. "He woke up." A smile spread across her face and her eyes misted. "He woke up a while ago. Briefly. The doc says that's a good sign." She bit down on her bottom lip and a tear slid from her eye and down her cheek.

For as long as Dante had known Roxanne, she'd never cried in front of him. To see her cry now was nearly his undoing. "Is he going to be okay?"

The doctor stepped forward. "As far as we can tell, he appears to be recovering. We're going to keep him a little longer to monitor his condition. If he continues to improve, he should be able to go home."

His mother smiled through her tears. "It's a miracle." She shook her head. "The news showed pictures of his truck and it's a wonder he's still alive."

"Where's Tuck?"

"Someone looking for me?" Tuck appeared behind him, carrying two cups of steaming coffee. He walked with a limp, but he was wearing jeans and a clean flannel shirt and, other than a few bruises on his face, looked like Tuck. He started to hand the coffee to Dante. "You look like you could use this more than I can. Other than a few bruises and scrapes, I'll live. What happened to you?"

Dante had forgotten the bruise at his temple until that moment. He shrugged. "I ran into the door in my apartment."

His mother's eyes narrowed. Amelia Thunder Horse had that keen sense and woman's intuition. She always knew when he was lying. For a moment she looked like she was going to call him on it, but then she noticed the woman standing behind him and raised her brows asking politely, "Are you with Dante or are you waiting to speak with the doctor?"

Emma opened her mouth to speak, but Dante jumped in before she could. "Mom, this is Emma Jennings." Rather than burden his mother with their problems, he blurted, "Emma's my fiancée. She's come to spend Christmas with us. I hope you don't mind."

The family converged on the two, shock in everyone's expressions, especially Emma's. But she recovered quickly, wiping the surprise from her face.

His mother enveloped Emma in a bear hug, her eyes wet with unshed tears. "Wow, this is a surprise. A much-needed surprise. After all the tragedy and worry…this is wonderful."

Julia took her turn hugging Emma. "Congratulations. I'm so happy for you two. I'm Julia, Tuck's wife."

"I'm Tuck, one of Dante's brothers." Tuck hugged her, looking over the top of her head at Dante, pinning Dante with his stare. "How come we haven't heard anything about her up until now?"

Roxanne shoved him aside. "I'm Roxanne, Pierce's wife. Nice to meet you."

Emma hugged one after the other, muttering her thanks, looking flustered, her cheeks bright pink.

His mother wiped another tear from her eye and sniffed. "This is all so sudden."

Dante slipped an arm around Emma's waist and pulled her up against him. "I know. Seems like only yesterday we met. But when you know, you know. Right, Emma?" He smiled down at her, praying she'd continue to go along with his ruse.

She looked up into his eyes and nodded. "That's right. You just know." She looked out at the people surrounding her and gave a shaky smile. "I hope you don't mind my showing up unannounced."

Amelia hugged her again. "Not at all. There's plenty of room at the ranch and I'm just so happy that Dante's found someone. I've been worried about him since his return from the war."

"Mom—" Dante took his mother's hand "—I'm fine. I have a great job with the CBP and I'm still flying."

"And now you have Emma." Amelia sighed. "All my boys will be happily married and giving me grandchildren."

The elevator door pinged behind Dante, and Sheriff Yost from Billings County stepped through and strode to Amelia, taking her into his arms. "Amelia, darling. I came as soon as I could get away."

Dante's back teeth ground together at the proprietary way Yost held his mother in his arms.

Tuck stepped forward, his fists clenched. "What's he doing here?"

Amelia frowned at Tuck. "It's all right. William came when I called. He's working with the Burleigh County sheriff and the state police to determine the cause of the accident."

Dante stiffened, his arm tightening around Emma. "I thought you said Pierce's brakes went out."

Amelia shot a glance at Tuck.

Tuck faced Dante. "We had the truck hauled to the forensics lab in Bismarck. A mechanic did a preliminary look at the brakes. They'd been cut almost all the way through."

"When?"

"We don't know." Tuck rubbed the back of his neck. Scratches and bruises stretched down his arm, his elbow skinned and raw.

Yost interjected, "I spoke with the mechanic myself. Since the brake lines weren't completely severed, it took a while before all the brake fluid leaked out."

"We didn't know until it was too late to do anything about it." Tuck's gaze went to the door of a room across from the nurses' station.

A nurse stood and walked their way. "If you could,

please move your family reunion to the waiting room. We don't want to disturb the other patients."

The group moved to the waiting room.

Dante glanced around the room, his gaze going from Tuck to Julia. "Where's Lily?"

Julia smiled. "When Tuck's supervisor heard he'd been in an accident, he and his wife came to the hospital. His wife is keeping Lily right now." Julia took Tuck's hand. "We were just about to leave to go pick her up now that Tuck's been released. We'd planned on going back to the ranch, but now that you're here…"

"Emma and I are headed that way."

"Then you'll want to get there before the weather," Yost said. "The reporters are predicting another twenty-four inches and whiteout conditions late this afternoon."

Tuck pulled Julia's arm through his. "If you're heading back now, I'd like to stay until Pierce comes out of it."

Dante nodded, his gaze shifting briefly to Yost and back to his brother. "I'd feel better if you stayed. I can check on things back at the ranch and over at the Carmichael Ranch, as well." The Carmichael Ranch was adjacent to the Thunder Horse Ranch. Pierce lived with Roxanne at her ranch when he wasn't on duty with the FBI in the Bismarck office. Maddox Thunder Horse usually handled the day-to-day operations of Thunder Horse Ranch while Roxanne ran the Carmichael.

"Thanks." Roxanne took his hand. "I'm not leaving here without Pierce."

Dante squeezed her hand. "I didn't expect you to."

Amelia wrapped her arms around him and hugged him. "Be careful getting there. I don't know what I'd do if another one of my boys gets hurt."

He kissed the top of her head. "I'll be fine. You guys

worry about Pierce. Emma and I will figure things out back at the ranch. I would like to visit Pierce before I leave."

"He's only allowed one visitor at a time for a few minutes only." His mother smiled apologetically at Emma. "You can stay here with us while he goes."

Dante left Emma in his mother's hands, walked across the polished tile floor to the room his mother indicated and pushed through the big swinging door.

Pierce lay on a hospital bed, his large frame stretched from the headboard to the footboard. Covered in wires and tubes, he lay still as death, his bronze skin slightly gray, cuts and bruises marring his face.

Dante had been to visit soldiers in worse shape, but seeing his brother hooked up to all the gadgets and monitors hit him hard. They'd already lost their father. This shouldn't be happening.

His own helicopter crash seemed insignificant since he'd walked away from it relatively unscathed. Pierce was strong and with the help of *Wakantanka,* the Great Spirit, he'd pull through. But a little prayer wouldn't hurt.

Dante closed his eyes and lifted his face skyward. *"Wakan tanan kici un wakina chelee,"* he spoke the words softly, feeling them in his heart and the hearts of his ancestors. May the Great Spirit bless you, Thunder Horse.

EMMA EXITED THE hospital at Dante's side, her head still spinning with the congratulatory words of Dante's family echoing in her ears. Pulling the hood of her jacket up around her ears, she waited until they got in the SUV before saying, "What was that all about?"

Dante twisted the key in the ignition and backed out of the parking space. "What was what about?"

A shot of anger burst through her. "Fiancée?" She didn't know why his lie was making her so mad. Perhaps it was because his family had welcomed her so openly and with such love…it made her mad to build up their expectations only to disappoint them.

His lips twisted and he shot a quick glance at her. "I'm sorry. It was the only thing I could think of that would keep my mother from asking too many questions about my appearance and why you were with me."

"So you told her we were engaged? I could think of a dozen other things we could have told her but that."

"It's only for the short term, just through Christmas break. Once Pierce is out of the ICU and is home and well enough, she'll quit worrying about him and we can straighten it all out."

"I don't like lying to your family." Emma glanced out the window at the bleak skyline. "Especially to your mother."

"I don't like seeing her cry," he said softly.

All the anger slid away as Emma recalled the tears in Amelia Thunder Horse's eyes and the shadows of worry over her sons' accident. If Dante had told her he'd been shot out of the sky, she might have had a heart attack or at the very least a nervous breakdown.

Emma sighed. "I guess you did the only thing you knew how. I wouldn't want to burden your mother more when your brother is in the ICU."

Dante reached across the console and squeezed Emma's hand and kept holding it for a while afterward.

She stared down at his big fingers clasped around hers, her chest tightening. "You have a nice family."

"Yeah."

"You and your brothers are close?"

"They'd do anything for me and vice versa." He turned to her. "What about you? Do you have siblings?"

"No."

"What about your folks?"

"Gone." Which was true about both. Her mother was dead and she had no idea where her father was.

"I'm sorry."

"Don't be. I'm used to being on my own."

"No one should be alone during the holidays."

She shrugged. "I don't mind." Which was another lie. She hated the holidays for just that very reason. As much as she tried to tell herself it didn't matter, watching others laughing and taking time off to spend it with their families had always been hard on her. She'd been happy to spend her weekends alone on the dig. Digging in the dirt meant she wouldn't have to spend her weekends in her empty apartment. Perhaps she'd get a cat for company.

They traveled in silence the rest of the way to the ranch. The weather held all the way up to the last turnoff leading up to the sprawling ranch house when the first snowflakes began to fall. It wasn't long before more followed, cloaking the sky. By the time Dante parked in front of the house, the wind had picked up, blasting the snow sideways.

"You can go on in," Dante shouted over the wailing Arctic blast. "I need to check on the foreman and the animals in the barn."

"I'll go with you." She zipped up her coat, pulled her hood over her ears and shoved her hands into warm gloves. The frigid wind stung her cheeks, making her blink her eyes. Snowflakes clung to her lashes in clumps.

"You should go inside. I can handle this."

"Please," she said. "I need to stretch my legs."

"In this?"

"You forget, I'm from North Dakota, too." She grinned and followed him to the barn out behind the house.

Several horses were out in a corral, their backs already covered in a thin layer of snow. They trotted along the fence as Dante and Emma approached.

Dante opened the gate and snagged the halter of a sorrel mare. "Think you can lead her into the barn?" he yelled into the wind.

Never having been around horses, Emma figured there couldn't be much to walking a horse into the barn. She reached up and slipped her gloved hand through the harness.

The mare jerked her head up, practically lifting Emma off the ground. She bit down hard on her tongue to keep from screaming and tugged on the harness, urging the horse toward the door to the barn.

Dante passed her, leading a big black horse that danced sideways, tossing its head.

Thankfully, the mare followed the black horse through the door.

Once inside, out of the wind, the horse settled into a plodding walk.

"You can let go of her, she knows which stall is hers," Dante said. "I'll get the other two."

"What can I do?"

"Fill two coffee cans with sweet feed out of that bucket." He pointed to the corner where two large trash cans stood. One had big block letters drawn on the side that spelled out SWEET FEED. The other had CORN, written in capital letters.

Taking two coffee cans from a shelf above the trash cans, Emma opened the sweet-feed bucket and filled the trash cans with the sweet mash of grain and corn and what else, she had no idea, but it smelled like molasses.

The horses already in their stalls whickered, stomping their hooves impatiently.

The barn door swung open and Dante entered leading two large horses. He took them to their stalls and came back to grab the two cans. He filled the feed troughs in two stalls and returned to fill the feed buckets with more grain for the other two horses.

"I didn't see the foreman's truck outside. I hope he gets back before the storm gets any worse." He glanced down at her. "Ready?" he asked, holding out his hand.

Emma nodded and took his hand. He had to push hard to open the door, the wind was playing hell against the barn.

Once they were outside, Dante closed the barn door and then took off at a slow jog toward the house.

The snow had thickened until she could barely see the large structure of the ranch house in front of her.

Dante led the way, holding her gloved hand. When they reached the house he twisted the doorknob on the back. It was locked. Tearing his glove off his hand, he reached into his pocket for his keys and unlocked the door, pushing Emma through first. He quickly stepped in behind her and slammed the door shut.

Emma stood in a spacious kitchen with a large table at one end and a big gas stove at the other. Red gingham curtains hung in the window over the sink, making the blustery winter weather outside look cheerful from the warmth inside. For all the beauty and hominess, something wasn't right.

As she raised her hand to push her hood off her head, she stopped and sniffed.

Dante must have sniffed it at the same time, his nose wrinkling as he unzipped his jacket.

"Gas," Emma said softly.

When Dante started to shove his jacket off, Emma's heart leaped. "Don't move!"

Immediately, his hands froze with his jacket halfway over his shoulders.

"You smell it too?" she asked. "If you take your jacket off, as dry as it is in here, it might let out a spark. My hood does it every time I push it back from my head."

"Good point." He glanced at her. "Get out."

"I'm not going without you."

"If something happens to me and you both, no one will be around to get help. Don't argue, just get out." He walked to the door, holding his arms away from his sides to keep the Gore-Tex fabric from rubbing together and potentially causing a spark.

Emma's lips pressed together. "Okay, but be careful. I'd hate for my brand-new fiancé to go up in flames before I get a ring out of it." Though her words were flippant, her voice quavered. She opened the door carefully and exited.

Dante left the door open, the wind blowing snow through the opening onto the smooth tile floor.

Emma hunched her back to the frigid cold and waited while Dante turned every knob on the stove and the one for the oven, as well. Once he'd secured the stove and checked the gas line into it, he left the kitchen, disappearing around a corner into the darkened house.

By the time he returned, Emma's teeth were chattering and her eyelids were crusted with snowflakes.

"It's safe now. I have all the exterior doors open and there's a good breeze blowing through."

Emma stepped in from the outside. Although she was out of the wind, she was still cold and shivering. The clouds had sunk low over the house, blocking out any light from the setting sun well before dusk. Darkness descended on Thunder Horse Ranch.

Dante pulled her out of the breeze blowing through the house and enveloped her in his arms. "I want to wait a few more minutes before I feel confident it's safe."

Leaning her face into the opening of his jacket, she pressed her cool cheeks to his warm flannel shirt.

He took her hands in his, unbuttoned his shirt and pushed them inside against his warm skin. He hissed at the cold but didn't remove her hands. "Warmer?" he asked.

She nodded, not certain she could talk at that point. Her teeth were still clattering like castanets.

After a good five minutes with the cold wind blowing through the house, Dante closed the back door and went around the house closing the rest, mopping the snow-drenched floor with a towel he'd grabbed out of the bathroom.

When Emma started to take off her jacket, Dante placed a hand over hers. "Wait until it warms up in here to at least sixty degrees."

Content to do as he said, Emma stuck her hands in her pockets and glanced around the kitchen. "Did you locate the source?"

His brow furrowed. "One of the stove's burners was left on."

Emma's gaze captured Dante's. The attacks on Dante's helicopter, the trailer incident, his brothers' cut brake lines and now a house filled with gas were all too close together. "Does that happen often?"

"Never. When my mother talked my dad into buying a gas stove, she promised she'd handle it with care and always turn off the burners. He didn't want a gas stove in the house, afraid one of us kids would light our hair on fire or something. Mom was cautious about the knobs. If she even suspected she might not have turned off the stove, she'd drive a hundred miles back to check."

"Could she have left it on when she rushed to the hospital after your brothers' accident?"

"Maybe, but not likely."

"Coincidence?" Emma asked, shaking her head before he answered.

"I think not." He glanced around the kitchen. "Julia had said something about Mom hiring a security team to set up surveillance around the house. She's had some incidents, as well." He nodded to the corner. "Looks like they've started the work but have yet to install the cameras.

Emma followed his gaze, noting where wires stuck out of the corners of the room.

Dante left the kitchen and strode through the rest of the house, moving from one room to another.

Emma followed. Wires stuck out of the walls in every common area and in the hallway.

"What kind of incidents were they having here?" Emma asked, trying to keep up with him, noting the homey decor and wood flooring.

"I don't know. I think she was afraid to say anything in front of my mother. I'd hoped to find out more from the foreman."

"But he's not here."

No, and Dante had a lot of questions for the man. Where the hell was he?

When Maddox had started traveling to his wife's country of Trejikistan, he and his mother had hired Sean McKendrick to manage the ranch in Maddox's absence. Amelia was capable of a lot of things, but it was a lot for a lone woman. Sean had proven himself knowledgeable about horses and cattle and a good carpenter when things needed fixing. And he seemed to have a good heart and a love for the North Dakota Badlands.

Dante stopped in the living room and glanced down at an answering machine. A light blinked three times, paused and blinked three times again.

He punched the play button and listened.

*"Mom, it's Dante. In case you've seen the news reports about the helicopter crash involving a border patrol agent, I'm okay. Yes, it was mine, but I'm not hurt. Call me when you get a chance. Love you."* He erased the message.

"Good thing you got home first," Emma said. "Or else the jig would be up."

The second message played. *"Amelia, Sean here. Had to go into Medora at the last minute to pick up some supplies and the Yost boy. If you get back before I do, the horses need to come into the barn before the storm hits."* Dante deleted the message and played the third.

*"Amelia, Sean again. Having troubles with the truck engine. Don't think I'll make it back to the ranch before the storm. I'll get a room at the hotel for the night and be back first thing in the morning. I'm putting a call into the Carmichael Ranch to have the foreman come over and take care of the horses."*

As he deleted the last message on the answering machine, the phone rang.

"This is Dante."

"Dante, I'm glad you're home. It's Jim Rausch from the Carmichael Ranch. Sean tells me he's stuck in Medora for the night and there's some horses needing put up before the storm."

"I've already taken care of them," Dante reassured the man. "How are things your way?"

"Everything's locked down. Looks like that storm's gonna last until sometime in the middle of the night. I just wanted to get everything in place so that I'm not out in the snow in my house shoes. How's Pierce doing? Your family make it back to the ranch with you?"

"No, they're staying in Bismarck, close to the hospital. Pierce is still out of it. Although he did wake briefly."

"Sorry to hear that. What about Tuck?"

"Banged up, but on his feet."

"Good," Jim said. "Glad he's okay. I saw in the news about your helicopter crash. I guess you're okay if you're at the ranch."

"I am. I left a message on Mom's answering machine about it, but since she hasn't been home, and she hasn't seen the news, I didn't bother telling her. She's got enough to worry about."

Jim snorted. "And then some."

"Tell me about it." If anything were happening at the Thunder Horse Ranch, news would have made it to the Carmichael Ranch. Though Pierce spent his weeks in Bismarck, he commuted to the Carmichael Ranch where his wife, Roxanne lived.

"There's been one accident after another. First the barn door fell off its hinges and nearly crushed your brother Maddox the day before he left with Katya. Three days later, the hay caught fire in the barn. Sean was able to put out the fire before it did any damage, but it was close."

"What do you know about the security system Mom's having installed?"

"Sheriff Yost's son has a security business. He's doing the work. From what Roxanne said, he's not finished."

"No, not even close."

"Roxanne tells me Maddox is cutting short his stay in his wife's country to come home early because of all that's been happening. Your mother tried to convince him she's fine, but none of us like what's happening. And now this crash with your brothers. It's enough to push a sane woman over the edge."

Exactly Dante's worry. "Thanks for the update."

"Glad you're there to take care of things. Let me know if you need any help."

"Thanks, Jim."

Dante hung up the telephone and stared across the floor at Emma. "I'm sorry to say, but I think by saving my life, you've walked into a bigger can of worms than we originally thought."

## Chapter Nine

Emma insisted on spending the night on the couch in the living room. Being alone in the big house with Dante made her uncomfortable. After being in the presence of his family and extended family, she found herself wishing she really did belong and that was a dangerous thing to do.

She had bad luck with families. Her father had left when she was a little girl. As a single parent, her mother had left her alone since the age of twelve so that she could save money on babysitting.

To survive, she'd learned to cook and do her own laundry and that of her mother's or it wouldn't have gotten done. Her mother worked her day job and a night job to keep her in a private school.

A month after Emma graduated from high school, her mother caught a staph infection at the nursing home where she cleaned rooms. Within two weeks, she'd died.

Completely alone at eighteen, Emma had depended on herself since. Too many times when the world seemed too harsh or the tasks too hard, she'd gone back to her rented room and cried herself to sleep. She'd have given her right arm to have someone hug her and tell her everything would be all right.

She'd completed her undergraduate degree working nights washing dishes at a local restaurant. Then she worked her way through her master's degree as a teacher's assistant. She'd captured the attention of the department head and was offered a teaching position when she completed her master's and went on to get her doctorate, determined that no matter what, she would always be able to support herself without working two jobs like her mother had.

All in all, she'd had a limited family experience, whereas Dante's family was almost storybook perfect. Lucky man.

Dante had gotten up before dawn, dressed and went out to tend to the animals, leaving Emma to dress and scrounge in the kitchen for breakfast. The refrigerator was well stocked with enough food to feed an army. A freezer in the pantry was full of what looked like a half a cow's worth of packaged beef, frozen homegrown vegetables and loaves of bread.

She supposed they had to buy in bulk when they could only get to the major grocery stores once every other month and maybe not at all during the fierce winters.

Whipping up a half a dozen eggs, she chopped onions, tomatoes and black olives and tossed them in a skillet, pouring half the eggs over the top to make an omelet.

When she had two plates loaded, the back door opened and a frigid blast of air slammed into her. "Holy smokes." She danced out of the draft and grabbed the pot of coffee she'd made and poured a cup full. "Sit. I have breakfast ready."

"Thanks." Dante stomped his feet on the mat to get the snow off his boots and sniffed the air. "Smells better than gas." He winked and shrugged out of his jacket, scarf, gloves and an insulated cap. "You don't have to wait on me, you know. My mother taught us boys to cook and clean dishes."

"I know. But I was up and it gave me something to do. Besides, it's just as easy to cook for two as it is for one."

"Thanks." He pulled out her chair and waited for her to sit, before claiming one for himself. Then he wrapped his hands around the mug of coffee and let the steam warm his face. "Heaven."

His appreciation of her efforts warmed her. "Have you heard anything about your brother?"

"As a matter of fact, my mother called late last night after you were already asleep."

Emma held her breath, praying for good news after all the bad.

"Seems Pierce woke up late last night demanding dinner." Dante smiled. "He'll be okay if he's already bellowing for food."

Emma let go of the breath she'd held, a weight of dread lifting from her shoulders. She'd never met Dante's brother, but she understood how horrible it was to lose a family member and she didn't wish that kind of loss on anyone. "Thank God."

"They hope the doc will declare him fit and cut him loose today."

"That soon?"

"He's already been up and they've moved him from the ICU. It's only a matter of time before they throw him out."

"That's good news."

"I got ahold of Tuck and told him what happened to us."

Her head jerked up. "Does he know we're not really engaged?"

"No, I didn't tell him that part. I figured it would be

hard enough to keep Mom from knowing about our crash without disappointing her about seeing her last son settling down."

"Now that your brother is going to be okay, shouldn't we tell her the truth?" The thought made her belly tighten and she set down her fork, no longer hungry. Amelia had been so happy at her son's announcement.

"No. Let her enjoy her Christmas. After the holidays, when everything settles down and we've figured out what the hell's going on, we can break it to her. She'd be better prepared to handle it then. Maddox will be back with his wife, Katya. Maybe they'll have a baby or something to keep Mom from worrying about me."

"Are they expecting?"

Dante laughed. "I wouldn't be surprised. And in the meantime, Tuck works for the FBI. He's going to put feelers out on the crash, the trailer demolition that almost included us and the explosives that took care of my Jeep."

Emma's lips quirked upward. "Must be handy having a brother in the FBI."

"Even handier to have two," Dante corrected. "Pierce is also in the FBI."

"Two FBI agents and a CBP agent. Don't you have one more brother? Is he in the FBI, as well?"

"No, he's the only one who stayed to be a full-time rancher."

Emma glanced around. "Then where is he?"

"He married Katya Ivanov, a princess from Trejikistan." He raised his hand. "It's a long story, which I'm sure they'd love to tell you all about over the holiday. They're visiting her brother in her home country and should be back soon."

"You have a very interesting family. How do you keep up with them?"

"Through Mom." Dante smiled. "She's the glue that holds us all together."

Having met Amelia Thunder Horse, she could see how. The woman was open, loving and cared deeply about her boys and wanted them to be happy. And she seemed to include their wives in her circle of love.

An ache built in the center of her chest and her eyes stung. To change the subject before she actually started crying, she swallowed hard and asked, "How much snow did we get?"

"It wasn't as bad as the weatherman predicted. We only got about a foot. We should be able to make it to town and collect the foreman and whatever supplies we might need."

"I think your mother's pantry and freezer are stocked for the apocalypse."

He laughed out loud. "Just wait. You haven't seen how much the Thunder Horse men can eat."

"If they're all as big as you, I can imagine."

Dante helped her clean the kitchen, proving his mother had taught him well. If he bumped into her more than he should have and reached over her, pinning her against the counter, it was only to get to the cabinet above.

Emma didn't read anything more into it than she dared. Dante Thunder Horse was a very handsome helicopter pilot, and he could do a lot better than dating a mousey college professor like Emma Jennings.

By the time they'd finished the dishes, she was flushed and her body oversensitized to his every touch.

"I'll be ready to go as soon as I brush my teeth." Emma hurried away to lock herself in the bathroom. The woman staring back at her in the mirror was a stranger. Her cheeks were full of color and her brown eyes sparkled. Even her dark brown hair was shinier. What had gotten into her? This was all make-believe and would end when the holiday was over.

The devil on her shoulder prodded her. So what did it hurt to live the dream for a few short days?

"A lot. It could hurt a lot," she whispered to the woman in the mirror.

Herself.

And Dante's mother when they finally told her the truth. But she'd support Dante in any decision he made, as any good mother would. She'd see that Emma wasn't the right woman for Dante and accept that it was a mistake.

The warmth of the woman's arms around her still resonated with Emma, and she missed her mother all over again.

She asked herself again, what would it hurt to pretend she was a part of this family, if only for the holiday? It would help Amelia get through it without more undue stress, Emma would have Dante and his family around her for protection and she wouldn't spend Christmas alone.

She ran a toothbrush over her teeth and made a solemn vow to herself not to lose her heart to a man that was still in love with a dead woman.

Splashing her face with water and then drying it on a towel, Emma squared her shoulders, hurried out of the bathroom and slammed against a solid wall of muscle.

Dante's arms came up around her to steady her on her feet. "Are you okay?"

Her breath lodged in her throat, her body tingling everywhere he touched it from her thighs to her breasts. "Yes." Emma's fingers curled into the fabric stretched across his chest. "Yes, I'm fine." Her pulse thumping hard in her veins, she straightened and stepped back.

"I was just about to knock and see if you were going to be ready anytime soon."

"I'm ready. All I have to do is grab my coat." *And pull myself together.*

"Wear your snow pants. It's extremely cold and windy out there."

"Okay." She hurried to the living room, jammed her legs into her snow pants and dragged them up to her waist, zipping and snapping them in place. Her boots went on next and finally her jacket. So much for being sexy in the morning with Dante. Dressed up like the Michelin Man, she looked like any other guy gearing up for the North Dakota weather. Puffy and shapeless.

"I'm ready." She crossed to stand in front of him, feeling lumpy and ugly.

A smile slid across Dante's face and he cupped her chin. "Anyone ever tell you that you're cute when you're all bundled up like the kid in *A Christmas Story?*"

She stared up at him, not sure if he was serious or just pulling her leg, surprised by the gleam in his eye and even more surprised when he bent to kiss her and whispered, "I missed you last night."

Before she had time to digest his comment, he turned and walked out the door into the cold, biting wind, stopping long enough to hold the door for her.

She walked through, still wondering why he'd kissed her and what he'd meant by his words.

THE DRIVE INTO Medora took twice as long as usual with the fresh snow and the unfamiliar vehicle. Dante didn't know the full extent of the little SUV's limits and wasn't willing to test them any more than he had to. He needed to get to town, pick up the foreman and do some asking around about what was going on in the area.

Maybe someone had information that would shed light on the happenings out at the Thunder Horse Ranch. He might also find out if the accidents were limited to the Thunder Horse family or if others in the area were having similar issues.

In Medora, Dante stopped at the diner, figuring Sean would probably hang out there with nowhere else to go until the truck was running.

He parked the vehicle on the main road running through town and helped Emma down. They entered the diner together. As he suspected, Sean was seated at one of the tables with a cup of coffee, a plate with a half-eaten biscuit and one of the biggest gossips in town sitting across from him. The local feed-store owner, Hank Barkley, knew as much, if not more, about everybody's business than Florence Metzger, the owner of the diner.

Sean stood when he spotted Dante and held out his hand. "Good to see you in one piece. I heard Pierce is feeling better."

Dante almost laughed out loud at the news.

Hank rose to his feet and shook Dante's hand. "Heard he was hollering for breakfast. He had us all worried." The man's inquisitive gaze fell on Emma and he asked, "Who do you have with you?"

"Emma Jennings." He introduced the men to her and asked, "Got room for two more?"

"Sure," Hank said. "We were just killin' time."

"Yeah, looks like we have until spring." Sean glanced out the window. "I don't think this batch of snow is going to melt until April."

Emma slipped out of her jacket and took one of the seats at the table. Dante sat in the chair beside her, his leg touching hers. Even through the thick snow pants and his insulated coveralls, he got a jolt. Something about Emma made his blood hum and his libido kick into overdrive. It had been a long night alone in his bed. Between getting up to check on her and lying in his bed awake but dreaming about making love to her, he'd slept little. A twinge of guilt accompanied these feelings. Memories of Sam were fading, which caused him more pain.

"Everything holding up out at the ranch?" Sean's words broke into his thoughts.

Dante nodded. "I took care of the animals before I left for town."

Sean and Hank sat across the table from Dante and Emma, each lifting his cup of coffee.

"Mack said he'd have to order a water pump for the truck and it would take a day or two for it to get in," Sean said.

"Then it's a good thing I came to get you." Dante glanced up at Florence when she stopped at the booth.

"Dante Thunder Horse, if you aren't a sight for sore eyes." The diner owner hugged him and looked over at Emma with open curiosity. "Is this the little filly you're engaged to?"

Emma's eyes widened.

Dante pressed a hand to her leg, his lips twitching. "Who'd you hear that from?"

Florence propped a fist on her ample hip. "I have a cousin working at the hospital in Bismarck."

Sean smiled. "I got the news from Hank."

Hank's chest puffed out, proudly. "Heard from Deputy Small, who got it from Sheriff Yost."

"I suppose the whole town knows by now?" Dante sat back and glanced at Emma.

Her face was pale and she gnawed on her bottom lip.

She hated lying to people and the more folks who knew, the more she'd probably consider she was lying to.

He draped an arm over her shoulders and leaned over to kiss her cheek. "The answer to Florence's question is *yes*. This is Emma Jennings from Grand Forks. My fiancée."

Sean, Hank and Florence all congratulated them at once, shaking Dante's hand and coming around the table to hug Emma, before resuming their original positions.

"That's just wonderful." Florence clapped her hands, her eyes shining. "Young love is so beautiful. But seriously, let me see the ring. You know it's all about the ring. It tells a lot about the man giving it."

Emma's face blanched even more, and then turned a bright red.

Dante hadn't even thought about a ring until that moment and he could see how uncomfortable Emma was with all the attention the lie had brought. "Shh, Florence, you'll spoil the surprise." He gave her a conspiratorial wink.

Florence frowned at first and then slapped a hand over her mouth. "Oh, yeah. Christmas is right around the corner."

Disaster averted, Dante took Emma's hand and held it in his like a newly engaged man would. Her fingers were stiff and cold. "But enough about us." Dante leaned his other elbow on the table. "What's going on around here?"

Hank and Florence were more than willing to fill him in on all the happenings of the small community. Frank and Eliza Miller had another baby. That would make five. Jess Blount and Emily Sanders got married a couple of months ago and were already expecting. Old Vena Bradley passed in her sleep last week, and her daughters aren't talking to each other because they can't agree on who gets what of the deceased's Depression-era glass collection.

Dante listened, bearing with the litany of social gossip, recognizing most of the names.

A customer at another table waved at Florence.

"I gotta get back to work. Yell if you need anything." She hurried off to pour coffee and deliver orders for the customers.

Turning to Hank, Dante asked, "How are things in town? Any new businesses or old ones that closed? Any new people you've seen around?"

"The Taylors finally sold their hardware store to a couple from Fargo. The old sawmill closed just before Halloween, and that abandoned hotel building sold to an investor from Minneapolis, and he's been renovating it." Hank paused to breathe, then launched into more. "I think it's because of the oil speculators who've been here off and on for the past six months, trying to buy up land."

"Same oil speculators that were here last summer?" Dante asked.

"Yes, and some new ones," Hank said.

Sean's brows furrowed. "Your mother didn't tell you about them? They've been out to the ranch several times, one in particular, that Langley fellow. He's bad about showing up whenever he likes. No matter how many times she tells him she's not selling the ranch or mineral rights, he keeps coming back. It's part of the reason she's having the security cameras and an alarm system installed."

Dante leaned forward. "What about the accidents out at the ranch? Do you think the speculators are responsible? Could they be trying to scare my mother into selling?"

Sean crossed his arms. "It would take a lot more than that to scare your mother into selling. She's feisty and doesn't let much slow her down." He chuckled. "That woman has more spunk than most eighteen-year-olds."

"But the ranch is a big responsibility for a lone woman, with Maddox gone a great deal of time," Dante observed.

Sean bristled. "I'm out there as much as I can be. I guess I could insist on her coming to town with me when I go for feed and supplies. I wouldn't mind the company. And those accidents could be just that—accidents. The barn door could have been working its way loose. You know how bad the winds are out here. And the hay was green when we put it in the barn. It could have caught fire due to spontaneous combustion."

Dante knew green hay could catch fire. That's why they usually were careful to let it dry before baling. He understood the hay had to be baled sooner because, after they'd cut the hay, a rainstorm had been predicted and they had to get it baled before the rain. "But to have two accidents like that in one week…" Dante shook his head.

The foreman shrugged. "The sheriff didn't find any evidence of tampering that could account for the door or the hay. We were just lucky no one was hurt."

"No footprints or fingerprints?"

"It rained late the night before the door fell. If someone loosened the hinges, it was before the rain. All footprints would have been washed away."

"What about the fire? Anyone out at the ranch that shouldn't have been?"

Sean's lips tightened. "Your mother was out on a date, and I was on my way back from the feed store when it started."

"Whoa, whoa, whoa." Dante held up his hand. "My mother was out on a date?"

Sean didn't respond.

But Hank did. "Sheriff Yost has been courtin' your mother. I've heard him say on more than one occasion that he wants to marry her. He told Florence he's been in love with Amelia since before she married your father, back when she sang in the *Medora Musical* in the summer."

"I didn't think she was that serious about the man."

"He's persistent," Hank said. "I'll give him that."

Sean scowled. "I don't know what she sees in him. She deserves better than that."

Dante studied the foreman. Something in his tone made him sound almost jealous.

Emma, who had been sitting quietly during the entire conversation, sat forward. "Are the oil speculators still in town?"

"Yeah. Some of them have rooms in the part of the hotel that's been newly renovated."

"What do you know about the security system Mom's having installed?" Dante asked.

"All I know is that Ryan, Sheriff Yost's son, started putting it in a couple of weeks ago, but he's waiting for some cameras that were back-ordered."

"I didn't know Ryan was back in this area. Didn't his mother take him to live on the Rosebud Reservation way back when she divorced Yost?"

Hank rubbed his hands together like a man staring at a particularly tasty meal. "I spoke with Ryan myself. He left the rez when he was eighteen, spent four years enlisted in the army, deployed to Afghanistan, got out and went to work as a security guard contracted to construction teams in Afghanistan for a couple of years. When he came back to North Dakota, he went to work for a man who installed security systems. About a year ago, his boss retired. Ryan took over this region for the security company. His territory is pretty much everything from Bismarck west. I think he's even got Minot."

"Is he based out of Medora?"

"For now. But he's on the road a lot. He even bought an old plane he uses to get back and forth faster. Got his pilot license so he can fly it himself."

"That boy seems to be doing something with his life," Sean said. "Not all of the boys from the rez are equally successful."

Dante knew that. His great-grandfather had moved off the reservation when he was old enough to leave. Though his heart remained with the Lakota people, he knew he had to get away to make a life for himself and his family.

"The boy doesn't look much like Sheriff Yost. Got more of his mother in him. Some of us wondered if he really was Yost's son. When his wife left him to return to the reservation, she didn't want anything to do with Yost, and Ryan never visited his father."

"Where is Ryan now?"

"I heard he had a job in Bismarck," Hank said. "Should be back later today. He's staying at the hotel they're converting. I think that's where the oil speculator is staying, as well."

Dante sat back, digesting all the information he'd been given. "Anything else going on around here that should raise some red flags?"

Sean grinned. "We'd like to hear more about what happened to you. We saw pictures of the crashed helicopter. You know it's only a matter of time before your mother finds out about it."

"Hopefully, by being here, she won't get upset. She'll see that I'm all right and let it go."

Sean grinned. "Don't bet on it. Amelia will be calling your boss to tell him you can't fly anymore."

Dante could imagine his mother doing that. Almost. She had never been happy about the danger her sons faced in their chosen career fields, but she respected their decisions and was as proud as any mother over her sons' accomplishments.

Pushing back his chair, Dante stood and held out a hand to Emma. "I have a few errands to run before I head back."

"Anything I can do for you?" Sean rose to his feet, as well.

"If you need feed, you might want to load some in the back of the SUV I rented. Emma and I will be back shortly and we can get back to the ranch."

"We could use more feed for the horses."

Dante tossed the keys to the foreman and helped Emma into her jacket. "Good to see you, Hank."

Florence passed by and he stopped her to give her a hug. "Good to see you, too, Florence. You're as beautiful as ever."

"Oh, now, Dante, you know how to make an old woman swoon." Her cheeks were flushed and she hugged him back.

Grabbing Emma's gloved hand, he made his way through the tables to the door.

Before Dante stepped out of the diner, his cell phone rang. The caller ID screen had Mom in bright letters. He answered, "Hi, Mom. How's Pierce?"

"The doctor's already discharged him. Can you believe it? I tried to get him to keep him for another day, but he said he was too disruptive to the hospital staff and that he'd be better off recuperating at home. We're already on the interstate and should be home in less than three hours, if the Great Spirit is willing and the roads stay clear."

"Who's driving?" he asked, knowing Pierce would hate letting someone else do the driving.

"Roxanne." His mother chuckled. "Pierce wanted to, but she told him to be quiet and lie down."

"What about Tuck?"

"He's headed home as well, but later this afternoon. He had some things he wanted to check on at his office. Then he, Julia and Lily will be on their way home for the holidays."

"What are you coming in?"

"We rented a four-wheel-drive vehicle for two weeks, or until the insurance company can make heads or tails out of what happened to Pierce's truck."

"Did you test the brakes?"

His mother snorted. "Tuck got under the hood, then under the car itself to check the brakes. He reported that everything looked serviceable. No leaking fluid or broken lines."

"Good. I'd like to have all of my family home for Christmas."

"Yes, and won't it be wonderful with everyone there. And now that you have Emma, our little family is complete and growing."

Dante's teeth ground together, but he held his tongue. Why ruin his mother's Christmas? She seemed thrilled that he'd found a woman to share his life.

His gaze shot to Emma walking beside him, her collar pulled up, her long brown curls whipping around her face. He was certain she didn't have a clue how beautiful she was.

She turned her head, catching him staring at her and she stumbled on the sidewalk. "What?" she asked.

"Nothing," he said. "I was just thinking how glad I am you decided to come with me. I hope you enjoy my family as much as they're sure to enjoy you."

Emma blinked up at him, long strands of rich chocolate hair dancing around her face. "You think they will?"

"Positive." He took her gloved hand in his and pulled her into the curve of his arm.

They walked the rest of the way to the little hotel which exterior looked brand-new. Once they entered the lobby area, Emma realized it still had a lot of work to go on the interior.

"May I help you?" a bored young woman asked.

"Can you tell me if Ryan Yost is in his room?"

"No." The woman smacked her gum, gave Dante a sweeping glance and smiled up at him. "I have empty rooms. Need one?"

Dante gave her his most charming smile. "Maybe."

## Chapter Ten

The young lady's face flushed with pleasure and she batted her eyes.

Emma's own knees weakened when Dante turned up the wattage on his smile. Normally dark and intense, when he smiled it changed his entire appearance.

In his photo with Samantha, he'd smiled like this. Emma found herself wishing she could bring back the happiness he'd felt before he'd lost the love of his life. What would it be like to be loved so completely by a man like Dante?

Dante leaned over the counter toward the blushing girl. "Nicole? Is that your name?"

She nodded. "Yes."

"Such a pretty name for a pretty girl."

Nicole pressed one hand to her chest and brushed her long blond hair back behind her ear. "Thank you."

"I'm—"

Nicole raised her hand. "Don't tell me. You're a Thunder Horse. I can tell by your features. You look a lot like Maddox."

Dante inclined his head. "That's right, Maddox is my brother. I'm Dante." He turned toward Emma. "And this is Emma. We're Ryan's friends," Dante said, twisting the pen on the counter between his long, dark fingers.

"It's been a long time since we've seen him and we just wanted to say hello."

"Oh, is that all?" Her lips spread in a smile and she played with the ends of her hair. "He's been living here since they got room 207 finished. But he's not there right now. When he left this morning, he said he wouldn't be back until around noon."

"That's all we needed to know." Dante straightened and winked at the girl. "If you have a pen and a little piece of paper, I could leave a note on his door to contact us when he gets back in."

Nicole immediately dug beneath the counter and surfaced a pad of sticky notes and an extra pen, scribbling something on the top note. "Will this do?" She slid the pad and pen across the counter.

She'd written her phone number on the top page and the words *call me* beneath.

"Perfectly." Dante winked again, gathered the items and looked around.

"The stairs are behind the potted plant." Nicole pointed to a fake ficus tree in the corner of the lobby. "First floor up, second door on the right."

"Thank you." He turned to Emma. "Do you mind waiting here, sweetheart? I'll only be a minute."

Her heart skipped a couple of beats at the endearment before she remembered it was all part of the ruse. "I'll wait here." Emma darted a glance at the blonde.

Nicole watched Dante disappear around the corner before she turned her attention back to Emma. The young lady's brows rose and her lip curled in a little sneer. "Dante's from here. I'd recognize the Thunder Horse name and those beautiful cheekbones anywhere." Her gaze slid over Emma. "But you must be new around here."

Emma nodded. "I live in Grand Forks. I'm..." She didn't know whether or not to announce that she was Dante's fiancée. The lie didn't come easily to her lips. "I'm here visiting the Thunder Horse family."

Her brows furrowing, Nicole tilted her head. "Is Dante the Thunder Horse brother that just got engaged?" Her eyes narrowed as she surveyed Emma anew. "Are you the fiancée?"

Damn, word spread like wildfire in the small town. "Y-yes," Emma acknowledged. Then she straightened her shoulders and spoke with more conviction. "It was so sudden. He surprised me yesterday with his proposal. I'm still getting used to the idea." Forcing a smile to her lips, she pretended to be the giddy bride. Okay, so he hadn't proposed, but had gone directly to announcing their engagement. But she had been surprised. "I was so shocked, I barely knew what to say."

Nicole snorted. "Obviously you said yes." Her gaze shifted to Emma's hand. "What? No ring? What a shame."

Emma's cheeks heated and she stuffed her hand in her pocket. "Not yet." She leaned forward, her voice dropping to a whisper as she used Florence's supposition. "Could be what he's planning for Christmas." There, it wasn't a complete lie. By the time the holidays were over, the engagement would be broken.

But for now, she could pretend, and Nicole could back off her flirting with Emma's pretend fiancé.

Two workmen entered the lobby carrying a heavy roll of carpet.

Nicole left her position and hurried down the hallway to open a door for them.

Two more men entered the lobby, both wearing suits

and expensive-looking trench coats. When they spotted Emma, the first man smiled.

"Well, what have we here?" The man stuck out his hand. "I'm Monty Langley, my partner here is Theron Price. And you are?"

Emma ignored the outstretched hand still encased in black leather gloves. "I'm Emma."

"Emma, Emma, Emma." The man leaned on the counter, his gaze traveling from the tip of her head to the snow boots on her feet. Glad she wore several layers of clothes, she raised her brows.

"Are you checking in to the hotel?" Monty asked.

"No."

"No? Well, would you care to have a drink with me later? I'm sure we can find a bar around here somewhere."

"No, thank you." She hoped he'd get the hint.

"Well darn, and here I thought things were looking up in this godforsaken little hellhole."

"I guess you were wrong." She smiled and turned away, watching his movements through her peripheral vision.

The man's eyes narrowed and he glanced at his partner. "Come on, Theron. I have a bottle of whiskey in my room." As he walked down the first floor corridor, he shot back over his shoulder. "And they say the people are friendly in North Dakota."

"To friendly people, not jackasses," Emma muttered.

"I heard that," Langley said.

Once the two men disappeared into a room down the hall, Emma took the opportunity to escape up the stairs to room 207.

Dante wasn't anywhere in sight, and the door to room 207 was slightly ajar.

She pushed through and entered. "Dante?" she whispered. The room was dark, the drapes pulled over the window. Clothes were strewn across the floor and bed, and the trash can was overflowing with empty food containers. She couldn't make out Dante's form in the shadowy interior.

A hand clamped over her mouth from behind and she was pulled back against a hard chest.

Emma's pulse leaped and she drew her arm forward to slam into her attacker's gut. Before she could, warm breath caressed her ear.

"Shh," Dante whispered, his lips brushing the skin beneath her earlobe. He dropped his hand to her shoulder and squeezed. "I'm almost done here."

"What are you doing?" she whispered.

"Looking around."

Was he crazy? "Isn't that breaking and entering?"

"Only if you get caught." Dante shrugged. "Besides, the door wasn't locked."

"Still, Nicole could come up and find you. Or worse, what if Ryan Yost were to walk in?"

"He hasn't, has he?"

"Yet. Langley and Price, the two oil speculators, showed up downstairs."

"Really? Maybe we should talk to them."

"I have no desire to. Langley hit on me."

Dante tipped her chin. "The man has good taste."

"We should leave now."

"And we will." He checked out the door, then dragged her out behind him. He closed the door and attached a sticky note to the outside.

Dante barely gave her time to read the note before he was tugging her down the hallway and the staircase.

Langley and Price hadn't come out of their room and

Nicole was still down the hallway with the workmen when Dante and Emma headed for the exit.

A dark-skinned man with a military haircut and piercing dark eyes pushed through the door before they could escape. His eyes narrowed for such a brief moment Emma almost didn't notice.

He stopped in front of them, blocking their exit. "You're one of the Thunder Horse brothers, right?" He held out his hand. "Ryan Yost."

Emma's heart dropped into her belly. It had been this man's room they'd been in. Had he arrived a minute earlier, he'd have caught them.

Dante gripped the man's hand and gave him a cool, calm smile. How could he act so nonchalant when Emma had to clench her hands into fists to keep them from shaking?

"Last time I saw you, you were a skinny little kid in the fifth grade," Dante said.

Ryan nodded, his lips curling into a smirk. "Yeah, that would have been right before my mother divorced the sheriff and we moved to the rez. Are you back in Medora for good?"

Dante shook his head. "No, I'm only here to visit family."

"Of course." Ryan glanced around. "Were you looking for me?"

"As a matter of fact, I was. My mother wanted to know when you might be back out to finish installing her security system."

"Right. I've been waiting for the cameras I ordered to come in. I expected them today, but apparently they were delayed. I should be out there tomorrow to install them."

"That's great. I'll let her know."

"I was surprised she wanted a system installed," Ryan noted. "Most folks around here leave their doors unlocked."

"Times have changed," Dante said.

"Yes, they have. It's been good for my business, anyway."

"I suppose so." Dante glanced toward the exit. "I better let you get back to what you were doing. We'll see you at the ranch tomorrow."

Ryan stepped aside, allowing them to pass. "You can count on it."

Back outside in the cold, Emma pulled her collar up around her neck. "What the hell was that all about?"

Dante's lips firmed. "Someone's trying to hurt the Thunder Horse family. I want to know who."

"You think Ryan Yost is the man behind it?"

"I don't know at this point. That's why I wanted to talk to him. Since he wasn't around and the door was unlocked, I thought I'd check out his living quarters and get a feel for the guy."

"I thought you knew him."

"He's a year younger than me. I knew him vaguely when we were in grade school, but, like he said, his mother divorced Sheriff Yost and took him to the reservation before he left the fifth grade. I haven't seen him since."

Dante grabbed her hand and headed back toward the SUV parked in front of the diner.

Sean was waiting inside and stepped out when Dante approached. "Ready?"

"Yup." Holding up his hand, Dante said, "I'll drive."

Sean tossed the keys and Dante caught them, hit the unlock button on the fob, then helped Emma into the passenger seat before going around to the driver's side. Sean slid into the backseat.

On the drive back to the ranch, Sean filled Dante in on other information about the happenings at the ranch.

"The wild horses have moved into the canyon. I spotted a mare with a limp. I think it was the one your brother calls Sweet Jessie. I'd like to get out there and check on her sometime today if possible and bring her back if she needs doctoring."

"She had a foal last spring, didn't she?"

"Yes. He's doing good on his own, but I'm worried about her."

"Perhaps I can help out." He turned to Emma. "Have you ever ridden a horse?"

Emma shook her head. "Sorry." Life on a ranch was so far out of her league. "Isn't it kind of cold to be out riding?"

Dante's lips twisted into a wry smile. "North Dakota ranchers don't get any breaks. The animals always come first."

"You're right." Nevertheless, a chill slithered down Emma's spine. "I'd like to go. Is it hard to ride a horse if you've never done it?"

Sean laughed from the backseat and Dante smiled. "The dead of winter might not be the best time to learn. If you want to go out with us, I could take a snowmobile. Sean will need to ride a horse in order to lead Sweet Jessie back if she needs tending."

Feeling inadequate, Emma felt the heat rise in her cheeks. "I don't want to slow you down."

"Not at all. If anything, we can get out to Sweet Jessie sooner than Sean and assess the situation. By the time Sean gets there, we'll have her roped and ready for him to lead her back, if need be."

Mollified, Emma nodded. "Okay. I would like very much to go, as long as I'm not in the way."

By the time they reached the ranch, Emma was feeling more relaxed around Sean and Dante, listening to their plans for what needed done before the next big storm rolled in.

When they drove up the driveway to the ranch house, Dante said, "Oh, good. The family made it."

Three vehicles stood out front—a shiny new SUV, a big ranch truck with knobby tires and a white SUV with the markings of Billings County Sheriff written in bold letters on the side.

Once again, her nerves got the better of her and she took her time climbing out of the vehicle.

"Looks like the sheriff arrived with them." Sean headed for the house ahead of them.

"What's he doing here?" Dante muttered as he climbed out. He walked around the side of the SUV, his face tight, and hooked Emma's elbow, leaning close. "Don't worry. My family doesn't bite…much."

"I'm not worried about teeth marks. I just don't like leading them on."

"As far as they're concerned, we're engaged. I don't see any need to tell them different."

"But it's a lie."

Dante stopped and faced her, holding her gloved hands in his, smiling. "If it makes you feel any better, I'll tell them we decided to hold off on the engagement so we can spend more time getting to know each other."

Emma sighed. "I would feel a lot better. Thanks."

Dante pulled her arm through his and walked with her toward the house.

Sheriff Yost emerged from the house as they walked up the steps.

The older man stuck out his hand. "Dante, glad you could make it home."

"Sheriff." Dante shook the man's hand. "I'm glad to be home."

"I just stopped by to see that your mother made it home all right." The sheriff plunked his hat on his head. "Well, I better get back to work."

Dante stepped aside, allowing the sheriff to leave.

Emma could sense the animosity from Dante. He didn't like the sheriff and didn't want him dating his mother. She understood. He probably felt it was a betrayal to his dead father.

The sheriff climbed into his SUV and backed out of the yard, turning down the drive to the gate.

"I just don't trust that man."

"Why?"

"I don't know. Gut feel, instinct. Something." He shrugged. "Come on, let's face the gauntlet."

Before Dante could grasp the door handle, his brother Tuck threw it open. "Dante, you sly devil, get in here." Tuck embraced Dante. "I was still out of it yesterday when you made your announcement. I didn't congratulate you properly." He hugged Dante again. "Julia and I are so happy for you."

"About that—"

Julia hooked Emma's arm and drew her into the living room. "Tuck's mother was so happy, she was beside herself. I think it was the only thing that got her through the day and into the night. She'd been so worried about Pierce, I think she was on the verge of a nervous breakdown. And then you and Dante arrive with your wonderful news and it perked her right up."

Emma bit her bottom lip, wanting to say something but at a loss for what words to use.

"Speaking of Mom and Pierce, where are they? Emma and I had something to say." Dante glanced around the room.

Roxanne emerged from the hallway, her face tired but happy. "Mom was so excited to have her brood home, I had a hard time convincing her that we could feed ourselves and that she needed to rest. She tucked Pierce into his bed and crawled into her own, too tired to argue."

"You should have been there last night," Julia gushed. "She had a dozen questions about your engagement. All the possibilities kept her mind busy so that she didn't have time to dwell on Pierce. And when Pierce woke up and found out you'd gotten yourself engaged, he almost left the hospital right then and there to come shoot you for not telling us all sooner."

Emma's heart had settled like a lump in the pit of her belly. With Amelia and Pierce exhausted from their ordeal and beyond their limits, Emma couldn't break it to them that her and Dante's engagement was a sham.

"About the engagement. It's not what you think..." Dante started again.

Julia, Tuck and Roxanne all turned toward him, smiling.

Emma took Dante's hand. "What Dante is trying to say is that it was all pretty sudden and we haven't even had time to get a ring."

"No ring?" Roxanne crossed her arms over her chest. "Isn't that how you ask a woman to marry you, by offering her an engagement ring?"

Dante glanced down at Emma, his gaze questioning.

"Tell them how you proposed, Dante." Emma smiled at him, giving him a subtle wink.

Julia clasped her hands together. "This is all so romantic."

Dante's eyes widened and then narrowed slightly. He faced his brother and two sisters-in-law. "Well, we haven't known each other very long, but I knew as soon as I met her that Emma was someone special."

Emma almost snorted. He'd had coffee with her and then run like a scalded cat, never to call her later. Feeling a little guilty, but somewhat vindicated, she waited with her brows raised to see what story he'd spin about asking her to marry him.

"Go on," Tuck said, smirking. "Tell us all how it's done."

"There really wasn't much to it. One minute we were just friends and the next minute I asked her to marry me."

"Seriously?" Roxanne crossed her arms. "Did you at least get down on one knee?"

Dante tugged at the collar of his shirt. "No. I just—"

"Blurted it out," Emma finished and took his hand. "It was so spontaneous and unrehearsed." Her pulse beating hard, she raised his hand to her cheek. "I can't imagine anything more romantic." And she couldn't, because she could never imagine anyone, especially Dante Thunder Horse, asking her to marry him. And he never would, for real.

"True love." Julia sighed. "Straight from the heart."

"That's right." Dante bent and kissed Emma's cheek.

"Come on, Dante, give her a real kiss," Tuck urged.

"Yeah, Dante, show us what got her to say yes."

Dante's jaw tightened.

Emma's cheeks burned. "Really, we're not that demonstrative in public," she insisted.

"The hell we aren't." Dante swept her into his arms and kissed her long and hard.

At first she was stiff and nonresponsive, too shocked by his move to think. But as his lips softened and moved over hers, she melted against his body. He traced the seam of her lips until she opened her mouth and his tongue speared through, caressing the length of hers.

Emma rose up on her toes, lacing her fingers around his neck. The world fell away and it was only him and her, alone.

"Ahem." Tuck cleared his throat. "You've made your point."

"What a kiss." Julia wrapped her arms around Tuck's waist and leaned into him.

Dante broke the kiss and leaned his forehead against Emma's for a moment. "Are you okay?" he asked.

She nodded, her tongue still tingling from the sweet torture of his.

Finally, Dante moved away and clapped his hands together. "Now, if you'll excuse us, Emma, Sean and I were headed out to check on Sweet Jessie."

"I'm coming," Tuck said.

"You were just in a car wreck," Dante said. "Give yourself at least another day to recuperate."

Tuck's brows rose. "I would think you'd need the recuperation time more than me."

"That's right," Julia said, lowering her voice to a whisper. "We saw the news clip on your helicopter crash."

Roxanne tilted her chin, staring closely at Dante. "We also saw an article in the morning paper about an explosion in Grand Forks that put one man in the hospital. Were you part of that, as well?"

Emma's cheeks heated. If they knew about the crash and explosion, how long would it take for them to figure out that she and Dante weren't really engaged?

Roxanne's eyes widened. "You were there!" She clapped a hand over her mouth. "That was your Jeep, wasn't it? That's why you're driving a rental."

Dante raised a hand. "It was an accident and neither Emma nor I were hurt in it."

"But you could have been," Tuck reminded him.

"I'd prefer Mom didn't know about the crash or the explosion," Dante said. "She's had more than enough drama for a lifetime."

Julia pursed her lips. "It's only a matter of time before she finds out. Nothing much gets by Amelia and she's tougher than you think."

"Look—" Tuck stepped into the fray "—we've all agreed not to say anything to Mom. But if she asks, we won't deny it."

Dante inhaled and let it out. "Fair enough."

"Now, do you want me to help you with the horses?" Roxanne offered.

"I'd go," Julia said. "But I'm not much good wrangling horses, and Lily's down for her nap with your mother. I hate to leave her."

"No." Dante held up his hand. "The three of us can handle this." He nodded to Roxanne. "And I'm sure Pierce will be looking for you when he wakes."

"It's supposed to drop down to minus twenty tonight," Tuck said. "Don't stay out past four-thirty when the sun sets."

As he headed for the door, Emma's hand in his, Dante called over his shoulder, "If we're gone any longer, send out a search party."

"Will do."

Dante stopped in the kitchen to swipe a handful of baby carrots from the refrigerator and stuffed them into the pocket of his snow pants.

While Sean hurried ahead to the barn, Dante hung back in the mudroom, making certain Emma had the right winter-weather gear on to ride on the back of the snowmobile. "Standing out in that wind is bad enough, riding on the back of the snowmobile is even colder."

"I'm tougher than I look," she assured him. Emma appreciated the extra care he gave her ensuring she would be warm enough, arming her with a warm wool scarf and heavy-duty insulated gloves and an insulated helmet.

When they reached the barn, Dante went in. An engine revved and he emerged minutes later on a sleek red snowmobile. Scooting forward, he jerked his head, motioning for her to climb on the back.

Glad she didn't have to stay at the house and lie to people she barely knew, Emma climbed aboard and wrapped her arms around Dante's middle. She liked being with him, even out in the frigid cold. And when they were alone together, she could be herself. No lies. She wished they could keep going.

## Chapter Eleven

Dante sped out of the yard as Sean led his horse out of the barn. Already past noon, clouds had accumulated in the western sky. The weatherman had predicted more snow that night. If nothing else, at least it would keep the saboteur from sneaking up on them and causing trouble. And if he did try something at night, he prayed the snow wouldn't hide his tracks.

Flying across the snow-covered prairie of the Badlands, he let go of the strain and pressure of the past couple of days. Out here, it was him, the sky and the incredible woman holding on to his waist. He could almost forget his life in the army, Sam and the other men of his unit.

He pushed aside the guilt of letting go. The cold reminded him of what was important—paying attention to the terrain and the time. If they were stranded out in the cold, especially near dusk, they might not be found until morning. Once the night got as cold as it would get, they wouldn't last until morning.

It took thirty minutes of steady riding to make it all the way out to the canyon. Without the added protection of foot and hand warmers, Emma's extremities would be getting pretty cold. He slowed the snowmobile and shifted her hands under his jacket, the cold gloves touching his bare skin made him jump. Unable to help her feet, he prayed the boots would keep her toes warm enough to ward off frostbite. He would have left her back at the house, but he wanted to keep a close eye on her. Not that he didn't trust his family, but they had their hands full and he figured she would have insisted on coming anyway.

When he finally made it to the edge of the canyon, he drove along the rim until he found the path leading down and stopped the snowmobile, shutting off the engine. "We walk from here."

Emma swung her leg over the back and swayed, holding on to the seat of the machine.

Dante got off and stood beside her. "How are your feet?"

"Cold. But not too bad now that we've stopped."

"I'll let you drive on the way back. There are hand and feet warmers for the driver."

"Now you tell me." She smiled. "No, really, I'm okay." She pulled off the helmet, laid it on the back of the snowmobile and secured her jacket's hood over her head. "What now?"

"We go down into the canyon and find the horses." He glanced down the path and back at her. "I should have warned you there would be hiking involved. If you're not up to it, you can stay here and wait for Sean."

"I told you, I'm tougher than I look. Lead the way."

He liked her spunky attitude and willingness to pitch in. For a college professor, she was a lot more apt and able than he'd originally given her credit. Still, it was a steep climb down into the canyon and even more difficult coming out on the snow and ice. If he saw that she was having any trouble, he'd turn back and get her out of the canyon.

They made it to the bottom with little trouble and the

sound of the snowmobile engine had alerted the wild ponies. They'd come to see if he had brought them treats.

Sweet Jessie, the tamest of the herd, led the way, favoring her right front leg with a decided limp, but no less determined to get to them ahead of the herd. She loved carrots and would follow him anywhere for the tasty treat. Especially in the dead of winter when food was scarce.

Her foal followed, his coat thick and fuzzy.

Emma's eyes widened. "They're so beautiful. Are they yours?"

"No, they're the wild ponies of the Badlands. They don't belong to anyone."

"Then why are you out here?"

"My family has always taken care of them, looking out for them and providing the Bureau of Land Management with an accurate annual count. When one is sick, we help if we can."

Dante pulled off his glove and fished in his pocket for the carrots. Already the cold wind bit at his fingers. When he had the carrots in hand, he gave half of them to Emma. "Hold these out in your hand."

"She won't bite me?"

"She might nibble a little, just keep your hand flat and she won't hurt you."

Emma held out her hand as he'd instructed, the carrots in the palm of her glove.

Dante slid his glove back on and kept his carrots out of sight.

Sweet Jessie trotted to within twenty feet of them and stopped.

"Why did she stop?" Emma whispered.

"She doesn't know you." Dante spoke softly to keep

from startling the other horses. "Give her time to learn you aren't a threat to her."

"She's so much bigger than I am. How could I be a threat?"

"You'd be surprised how threatening humans can be to the wild horses."

Sweet Jessie inched forward a little at a time, her neck stretching, her nostrils flaring, steam rising from her nose with each breath. When she was within three feet of Emma, she lifted her chin and nuzzled the carrots out of Emma's gloved hand.

Emma let out a soft gasp, a smile spreading across her face as she glanced up at Dante.

In that moment, the sun broke through the clouds and shone down on her face. Her dark hair framed her cheeks, the cool air making them rosy. But it was the flash of teeth and the excited gleam in her eyes that hit Dante like a punch to the gut.

Emma Jennings was a beautiful woman. So full of life, so innocent in many ways and strong and daring in others. This was the woman who'd ridden her snowmobile straight into danger to save him and then had given her virginity to him in the middle of a blizzard.

He reached for her, without realizing that was what he was doing.

Her smile slipped from her lips and her eyelids drifted halfway closed, her lips puckering slightly to receive his kiss.

In the frigid cold of the North Dakota Badlands, Dante Thunder Horse found himself on the slippery slope of possibly falling for a woman he'd only been around for a grand total of four days.

He pressed his lips to hers, taking them slowly at first. But as he deepened the kiss, his hunger grew and he crushed her to his body, frustrated by the amount of clothes standing between them.

Emma lurched, knocking into him and the moment was lost.

Sweet Jessie, impatient with their kissing, had sniffed out his other stash in the palm of his hand. The one fisted and holding Emma close.

The mare nudged him again, pushing Emma against Dante.

He laughed and set Emma to the side, offering the carrots up to the horse.

While Jessie's lips snuffled for the treat, Dante reached up and wrapped his hand around her frayed halter.

When the last of the carrots were gone, Sweet Jessie tossed her head, trying to loosen Dante's hold on her.

"You might want to step back," he told Emma.

She slipped from his arms and pressed a gloved hand to her swollen lips, her eyes bright and shimmering in the fleeting sunlight.

Dante held tight to Sweet Jessie, refusing to let loose.

After several attempts to shake him off, Jessie nuzzled his jacket, looking for more carrots.

Dante smoothed a hand over Jessie's nose and spoke softly. "Emma, could you hand me the lead rope?"

Emma scooped the rope from the ground and laid it across his open palm.

He snapped the lead on one of the metal rings in the halter. "Come on, Sweet Jessie. Let's see what's going on." He edged closer and pressed his shoulder to hers, then eased down to the leg she'd favored as she'd trotted up to them.

At first, she refused to let him lift the hoof. As he leaned harder against her, she shifted her weight to the other foot and he was able to raise the injured one.

As he'd suspected, the tender pad of her foot had been cut, and was infected and swollen with pus. She needed it drained and to have a poultice applied. And she needed to be kept in a clean, dry environment until the injury was well on its way to healing.

"Is it bad?" Emma asked.

"If we leave it alone, it might heal on its own."

Emma frowned. "And if it doesn't?"

"The infection could spread and she might die."

"Are we going to take her back to the barn?"

"That's what Sean will do when he gets here." Dante straightened and glanced up at the path. "You should go first. I'm going to lead Sweet Jessie out. I don't want you to be in danger if she spooks and tries to break away."

"Okay." Emma turned toward the path and started up the hill, climbing with quick, measured steps, pacing herself for the steep ascent out of the canyon. Every few steps she glanced over her shoulder to make sure Dante was still behind her.

Holding the halter in one hand and the lead in another, Dante led the horse up the narrow trail.

Every time rocks skittered down the slope, Emma's pulse leaped and she swung around, only to see the man and horse steadily climbing behind her.

Halfway up the hill, Emma was breathing hard, but confident she wouldn't have to stop before she made it to the top.

Head down, eyes forward, she took another step.

A loud blast cracked the frigid air and the earth beneath her feet shifted; gravel slid over the edge of the path and tumbled down the hill.

When she glanced up, the entire hillside seemed to be sliding downward toward her. "Landslide!" she cried out and turned back.

Sweet Jessie reared and nearly knocked Dante over the side of the trail. He let go of the lead and dropped to his knees.

The horse spun, lost her foot and slipped a hoof over the edge before she got her balance and raced back down the hill.

Higher up and closer to the source of the landslide, Emma knew she wouldn't get out of the way fast enough. When the wave of sliding rock and gravel hit, her feet were swept out from under her and she slid down the side of the steep slope, bumping and slamming against every rock, boulder and stump along the way. Pain ripped through her arms and head as she rode the wave of earth to the bottom of the steep precipice and slid thirty feet along the base of the canyon before the world stopped moving.

Gravel and small rocks continued to pelt her as she lay still, counting her fingers and toes and flexing her arms and legs. Everything seemed to be working okay, so she sat up.

"Emma!"

Emma shifted her head and glanced up.

Thankfully Dante had been farther to the north of the source of the landslide, the trail he'd been walking on had been spared. But if he didn't slow down in his race to the floor of the canyon, he'd end up causing a landslide of his own.

"I'm okay," Emma called out, the sound barely making it past her lips. Had she not been so bundled in snow pants and thick clothing, she might have more cuts and broken bones.

She rolled to her side, starting to feel the bumps and bruises she'd acquired in her pell-mell slide down the canyon wall.

"Don't move," Dante yelled. "You could have a spinal cord injury."

Ignoring him, Emma pushed to her hands and knees and stood. Her ankle hurt and she'd be a mass of bruises, but she was alive.

Dante arrived at her side, his dark face pale, his eyes wild. "You shouldn't have moved." He pulled her into his arms and held her. "Thank the spirits, you're alive." He continued to crush her to his chest, his arms so tight around her she could barely breathe without pain knifing through her.

"Careful there, Dante, I think one of my ribs is broken."

"Is that all?" He laughed, pushed her to arm's length and smiled down at her, running his hands through her hair, brushing the dirt off her face. He cupped her cheeks in his palms and bent to touch her lips with his. "You scared me."

"I scared you?" She chuckled, wincing with the effort. "I was pretty scared myself." She glanced around. "Where's Sweet Jessie?"

"Probably halfway to Fargo." He hugged her again, more gently this time, and then frowned, his gaze shooting back to where the trail had been. "What I want to know is how that landslide started in the first place."

Dante scanned the rim of the canyon above, searching for movement. Nothing but a few pieces of loose gravel moved between him and the top. Based on the loud crack he'd heard before the ground shifted, someone had set off a small explosion that started the landslide that almost killed Emma.

His jaw tight, anger rippling through him, Dante slipped an arm around Emma's waist and draped hers over his shoulder. He moved her to a safe location in the shadow of a huge overhang of solid rock.

"I'm going up to get the snowmobile."

"I didn't think you could get it down the trail."

"Not that trail, and definitely not now. But there's a wider one farther along the top of the canyon. I didn't want to bring it down here and have the noise frighten the horses."

"But that's already happened with the noise and the falling rock."

"Will you be all right staying here for a few minutes by yourself?"

She nodded, a shiver shaking her frame.

Dante needed to get her back to the ranch. Even though she hadn't had any major breaks, with a fall as frightening as that and all the bruises she'd probably acquired, she could go into shock. He hated leaving her, but it would take longer for him to carry her out of the canyon than to climb out and come back for her on the snowmobile.

"Go. I'll be okay." She wrapped her arms around herself and pulled her hood close around her face and smiled.

Dante ran across the rocks, headed north to the trail he knew was farther along the steep sides of the canyon walls. Hidden by a huge boulder, it was hard to spot until he passed it.

Soon he was on his way up the wider trail, breathing hard and worried about leaving Emma in the canyon.

What seemed like an hour later, he emerged on the rim of the canyon and glanced around for the person responsible for causing the landslide.

Nothing stood out on the flat landscape except the snowmobile he'd arrived on. He hurried toward it, praying whoever had set off the landslide hadn't damaged the snowmobile or wired it for explosives.

Desperate to get back to Emma before she went into shock, he shifted to sling his leg over the top and stopped short. Something stuck out from beneath the hood of the engine compartment. It looked like a strip of black electrical tape. Careful not to apply undue pressure, he lifted the hood and stared down at what looked like a lump of clay with a mechanical device stuck in the middle. A wire led from the device to the vehicle's starter switch.

He'd seen C-4 explosives before, but not on a snowmobile. The way he saw it, he had two choices. He could walk away and leave the snowmobile out there and wait for Sean to arrive on horseback. That would mean putting Emma on the back of the horse to transport her to the ranch at a very slow pace while one of them stayed out in the cold until help could return. It would be dark soon and the temperature would drop rapidly.

Or he could take his chances, disarm the bomb and be on his way. He studied the mechanism and the wire leading to the starter. It looked like the electrical charge from the starter would be the catalyst to detonate the bomb. If he pulled the wire off the starter wire, it should disarm the bomb.

Then again, he wasn't a bomb expert and he could blow himself up if he wasn't careful.

Dante stared out across the land and there was no sign of Sean. He sent a prayer to *Wakantanka,* reached in, gripped the wire and pulled it loose. Blessed silence met him and he released the breath he'd been holding.

Carefully, so as not to bump the C-4 and the device, he lifted it off the engine and walked a hundred yards away from the snowmobile and set the explosives on the ground. When he returned to the snowmobile, he checked the ground for tracks.

Another snowmobile had been there, one with a

chipped track. There was also a dark spot on the snow. He touched it with his finger and lifted it to his nose. Oil. The machine had been leaking oil.

Too worried about Emma to look further, he hurried back to his vehicle and went over it one more time with a very critical eye. Confident he hadn't missed another cache of explosives, he climbed on, grit his teeth and hit the starter switch. The engine roared to life. Shifting into forward, he drove the vehicle along the rim of the canyon to the wider trail leading down to the bottom.

Emma was hunched over at the base of the overhang where he'd left her. Her cheeks were pale and her lips were turning blue. "Come on, sweetheart." He helped her onto the seat and climbed in front of her. "Can you hold on?"

"I'll do my b-best," she said, her teeth chattering so hard it shook her entire body.

Slowly, he climbed the trail out of the canyon, holding on to her arm with one hand, steering the snowmobile with the other. When they reached the top, he realized Sweet Jessie had followed.

Dante left Emma on the snowmobile and tied the lead rope to the back of the vehicle. Moving slowly enough the horse could keep up on her sore hoof, he limped toward the ranch, a little at a time.

Fifteen minutes into their long trek back, snow began to fall. Out of the snow and clouds, Sean appeared on horseback.

Dante gave him a brief rundown of what had happened, speaking quietly enough so that Emma couldn't overhear him. Then he passed Sweet Jessie's lead rope to Sean and climbed onboard the snowmobile.

Emma leaned into him, her arms not nearly as tight, her face frighteningly pale. Dante drove as fast as he could without losing Emma off the back and pulled up in front of the house.

Rather than beep the little horn and upset his mother or brother, Dante dismounted, gathered Emma in his arms and carried her into the house.

Tuck met him at the door. "I thought I heard the snow-mobile." When he saw Dante was carrying Emma, he moved back. "What happened?"

"Trouble," Dante said. "I'll tell you all about it once I get her warm and dry. Is Mom awake?"

"Dante?" His mother appeared behind Tuck. "Oh, dear. What's happened to Emma? Did she fall off the back of the snowmobile?"

Dante's teeth ground together. "No, she slid into the canyon on a landslide. Someone call the sheriff."

## Chapter Twelve

She must have passed out on the way back to the ranch house. Once inside, the warmth surrounded her and she swam to the surface, nestled in Dante's arms, a crowd of his family gathered around. Immediately embarrassed at being the center of attention, she struggled weakly against Dante's hold.

"I can stand on my own," she insisted. "Please, put me down."

"Not happening," Dante responded.

"Want to lay her on the couch?" his mother asked.

"No, she's been through too much, riding a landslide all the way to the floor of the canyon."

"Wow, and no broken bones?" Tuck shook his head. "She's tough. Emma, you'll fit right in around here."

"Thanks," she said, her heart warming along with her cheeks.

"Yeah, well, I can't tell if anything is broken until we get her out of these clothes," Dante said.

"Nothing's broken," Emma maintained. "Put me down. I can take care of myself."

Dante's mother clucked her tongue. "Now, Emma, sweetie, you're practically family and you've been hurt. Let us fuss."

"You've already had more than your share of injured

family. You don't need to worry about me. Pierce needs you more."

"Someone call my name?" Pierce Thunder Horse appeared in the hallway holding an ice bag to his forehead.

"Pierce, what are you doing out of bed?" Roxanne hurried toward him, grabbed his arm and tried to steer him back down the hallway.

"I'm just fine, except for this knot on my head." He removed the ice bag to display a goose egg–size lump on his forehead along with several other cuts and bruises and a black eye.

Emma felt like *he* looked and she almost laughed, but couldn't because her ribs hurt and her lip was split. "If you'll put me down, I'll crawl into a shower and bed."

"Dante, honey, carry her to the bathroom. I can help her out of that snowsuit and into a nice warm bath."

At that moment, a warm bath sounded like heaven. Emma almost cried.

"I'll take care of her," Dante said.

"I'll get her some hot cocoa, painkillers and warm a blanket." Amelia whirled away.

The remaining members of his family and extended family stepped aside to allow Dante down the hallway. Too exhausted to argue, Emma leaned her cheek on his chest and closed her eyes.

"I'm going to set you on your feet. Think you can stand?" Dante asked.

Emma opened her eyes to discover they were in a bathroom with marble counters and a big mirror. One look at her wild, tangled hair and she groaned. "I'm a mess."

A chuckle rose up his chest and shook against her body. "How are you supposed to look after falling off a cliff?"

She sighed, tilting her head toward the mirror. "Better than this."

"I happen to think you look great. Here, let me have your coat." He unzipped the insulated jacket and eased it off her arms. "Okay so far?"

She smiled. "So far so good." Reaching for the waistband of her snow pants she tried to unzip them, her fingers fumbling with the zipper.

"Let me." He took over, sliding the zipper down and then shoving the pants off her legs, leaving her standing in jeans with her thermal underwear beneath.

Emma closed her eyes again and laughed. "Nothing says sexy like nine layers of clothing and thermal underwear."

Dante removed the jeans, slipping them down over her long johns "I happen to find women in thermal underwear very sexy." As if to prove it, he skimmed a hand along the side of her legs from her calves all the way up the outside of her thighs as he rose from helping her out of her jeans. When he straightened, he rested his hands on her hips. "Ready to take off the rest?"

Exhaustion disappeared as a blast of adrenaline-powered lust ripped through her, making her pulse race and her blood burn through her body.

"Shower or bath?" he asked, his hand on the hem of her shirt.

The tub was barely big enough for one person to stretch out, but plenty big enough if they stood. "Shower."

She lifted her arms, grimacing at the twinge of pain in her ribs. Her shirt and undershirt slid up over her head and then was dropped to the floor.

Dante turned to switch the water on in the shower and adjusted the temperature. Then he helped her out of her thermal underwear. When she finally stood in nothing but her bra and panties, Dante's gaze swept over her from head to toe.

"Oh, baby, you really did get beat up."

It wasn't what she wanted to hear. His words only meant she looked like hell.

But he bent to kiss a bruise on her shoulder that was already turning a deep shade of purple. He shifted to kiss another bruise on her arm, and across to press a kiss to the swell of her right breast where a strawberry mark indicated yet another.

"They don't hurt," she assured him.

When he straightened and stared down at her, Emma's heart sank.

"Much as I'd love to kiss you all over, you need your rest."

"I'm okay, really." Afraid she might sound too needy, she tried to reach behind her to unhook her bra and winced.

Dante turned her around and flipped the hooks open.

Her breasts spilled free and she let the straps slide down her arms. "Join me," she whispered.

His hand slid up her arms and cupped her cheeks. "Not tonight. I couldn't bear it if I hurt you more. I really think we should take you to Bismarck to the hospital and have them look you over."

Emma shook her head. "I'm only bruised."

He stared hard at her, his eyes narrowed. Finally he sighed. "You're very tempting, do you know that?"

She shook her head.

"But you've been through hell." He backed toward the door, his lips firming into a straight line. "Get in there and get your shower while I find something for you to wear."

Emma slid out of her underwear in front of him. Still,

he didn't take her up on the invitation. Instead, he turned and walked out, closing the door firmly behind him.

Disgruntled and too tired to do anything about it, Emma stepped behind the shower curtain, washed and rinsed her hair and ran a soapy washcloth over her entire body until she had all the grit washed away.

When she stepped out of the shower to dry off, a flannel pajama top lay on the counter. The top was big enough to fit several of her in it. She lifted it to her nose and sniffed. It smelled like Dante. Quickly slipping into it, she discovered why there were no pants to go with it. The shirt hung down past her buttocks and halfway down her thighs. A pair of her panties and her brush lay beside the shirt. Soon, she had brushed the tangles out of her hair and was dressed enough to leave the bathroom and step out into the hallway.

Several doors lined the wall. Dressed in nothing more than a big shirt, she didn't feel up to facing the family, but she didn't know where else to go but the living room where she'd slept the night before.

"Oh, good, you're out." Amelia appeared at the end of the hallway. She hurried to Emma's side and wrapped an arm around her waist. "Come on, let's get you into bed. I'm sure you're past exhausted."

Hustled to the second door on the right, Emma went with the woman, thankful she didn't have to face the rest of the family. All she wanted was a big painkiller and a really soft bed.

And if she had all her wishes…Dante lying beside her, holding her.

Amelia flung open the door and ushered her into the room. The bed was a big four-poster with a goose down comforter and a handmade quilt folded at the foot of the bed. The blankets were pulled back and crisp white sheets beckoned to her.

"Climb in, sweetie. There's a glass of water on the nightstand and a couple of pain pills to ease your discomfort."

"Thank you." Emma crawled into the bed and lay back on the pillows.

Amelia tucked the blanket around her and smoothed her damp hair back from her face. "You poor thing. What a way to start your visit on the ranch. Don't be too put off. It's not always so crazy around here. We go for years without any excitement."

Emma touched the woman's hand, a wave of longing washing over her. She missed having a mother and being taken care of. If she wasn't careful, it would be too easy to get used to it. "I'm sure it's lovely."

"There now, get some rest."

"Mrs. Thunder Horse?"

"Please, call me Amelia. All my daughters-in-law call me that."

A guilty twinge lodged in her throat. Emma swallowed hard. "Where's Dante?"

"Sean got back with Sweet Jessie. He and Tuck are helping doctor her hoof."

"Oh, good."

"He'll be in as soon as they have her settled." Amelia turned out the overhead light, leaving the lamp lit on the nightstand. "If you need anything, just yell."

"Thank you, Mrs. Thunder Horse."

She smiled. "Amelia. Please, call me Amelia. 'Mrs. Thunder Horse' is a mouthful."

"Amelia," Emma complied, liking the woman's open friendliness.

When Dante's mother left her alone, she took the pain

pills and washed them down with water, then lay back, wishing she felt good enough to go out to the barn and watch as they helped the injured horse.

She assumed she was in Dante's room. The sheets smelled like him and the decor was subtle shades of blues and browns. Very masculine, yet homey.

Several pictures lined the walls of Dante and his brothers at various ages. One was of all four boys holding up fishing poles and their catches. Another was of Dante, rifle in hand, kneeling on one knee next to what appeared to be a mule deer he'd bagged. He had a serious look on his face, but she could see the happiness and triumph in his eyes.

The last picture was of Dante wearing army dress blues, his back straight, shoulders squared, hair short and an American flag in the background. He looked proud, and so handsome Emma's heart pounded.

As the time passed, her pulse slowed, her eyelids drifted closed and she wondered where Dante would be sleeping when he finally came in.

DANTE DRAGGED HIMSELF into the house well after ten o'clock. The sheriff had come and Dante gave his statement about the explosion, the landslide and the explosives he found in his snowmobile. Once Yost left, Dante, Sean and Tuck had spent the next couple of hours working in the barn with the injured mare.

Sweet Jessie had been spooked about being herded into a stall when she'd been used to roaming the plains free. They had finally given her a mild sedative so that he and Sean could work on her sore hoof pad while Tuck held her head. Once they'd drained the abscess, they applied a poultice, gave her feed and water, and watched for a while to ensure she didn't kick the poultice loose.

All the while he'd been concentrating on healing the horse, Dante pushed what had happened that day in the canyon to the back of his mind.

Now that he was done and on his way back to the house, memories of the day flooded him. The one that stood out most in his mind was of Emma tumbling down the very steep wall of the canyon all the way to the bottom.

He hurried into the house.

His mother met him in the kitchen with a plate of food and a mug of coffee. "She's in your bed, asleep. You might as well eat and shower."

Tuck and Sean joined him at the table and he gave them the more detailed description of what had happened, and about the explosives still sitting out on the plains. By the time the sheriff had arrived at the ranch house, darkness had settled in and the snow was falling in earnest. He'd determined it was too dangerous to go hunting for explosives that could be buried under the snow by now. Especially in the dark. He'd call the state police and ask for the assistance of a bomb-sniffing dog. Hopefully, they'd get out there the next day and retrieve the explosive device before anyone else was hurt.

"Want me to call in the FBI bomb squad?" Tuck asked.

Dante considered his offer. "It might not be a bad idea. Is there any way to trace the C-4?"

"Not if they pulled all the packaging off it before deploying it."

Dante shook his head. "It was all clay."

"Maybe we can pull fingerprints from the clay, the detonation device or your snowmobile."

"Did you run the names I gave you by your guys at the bureau?" Dante asked.

"They're conducting a background check on Monty

Langley and Theron Price, the two speculators Hank mentioned, I'm having them run a check on Ryan Yost, the sheriff's son. I haven't heard anything yet."

"Yost has a plane. Have them run a check on flight plans in and out of Grand Forks." Dante's hand tightened around his coffee mug. "We have to find who's doing this before someone gets killed." Especially if that someone was Emma. "I think it's pretty apparent that whoever's doing this is targeting the Thunder Horses."

Tuck nodded. "Unfortunately, Emma was collateral damage."

That's what had Dante worried. "Who else is going to be caught in the cross fire until we resolve this situation?"

"I don't know, but I'm as afraid for Julia and Lily as you are for Emma. I keep wondering if I should send them away until all this dies down."

"What about your mother?" Sean added. "She's liable to get hurt, too."

Amelia entered the room. "Who's liable to get hurt?"

Sean leaped to his feet and offered her his chair. "Please, sit."

"Thank you." She smiled up at him as she took the seat. "You're such a gentleman."

Sean winked at her. "I only offer my seat to beautiful women."

Dante was stunned to see his mother's face flush a pretty pink. It made her appear twenty years younger.

She jumped right into their conversation with "Are you three talking about all that's been happening?"

"Yes, we have," Tuck said. "We think you and the ladies should leave the ranch until this situation is resolved."

She glared at the men. "I'll do no such thing. This is my home. I won't be run out of it."

"Amelia, we don't want you hurt," Sean said. "We think the boys are being targeted for some reason. The women might get caught in between."

"Well, I think it's up to us to decide what we want to do about it." Dante's mother lifted her chin and challenged the others with a pointed stare. "I've lived more than half my life here on this ranch. I won't be bought out, sold out or forced off by anyone. This little piece of heaven is my sons' heritage. Their father and I held on to it for them."

"Nothing's worth losing you, Mom," Dante said. "Or losing Emma."

"Or Julia and Lily," Tuck said.

"Or Roxanne," Sean added.

"I'm not going anywhere," Amelia stated. "So what are we going to do about this?"

Dante chuckled. "We got our pride from our father, but we got our fierce determination from you, Mom."

"Darn right you did." Her stern expression dissolved into a worried frown. "I hate seeing my boys injured. We have to put a stop to this. If only we knew who was doing it."

"And why." Dante pushed away from the table and stood. "Right now, I'm going to get a shower and then I'm going to check on Emma. Do you think we should take shifts through the night?"

Sean nodded. "I'll take the first one. You've been through a lot these past couple of days. Get some sleep."

Dante shot a glance at his mother to see if she reacted to Sean's statement.

Amelia crossed her arms over her chest. "If you're wondering whether or not I know about your helicopter crash, rest assured. I do. I've known since shortly after you visited Pierce in the hospital. You know a thing like that can't be kept a secret."

"I'd hate to know what other so-called secrets you know."

"I know more than you think. I might be getting older, but I know when my sons are keeping things from me." She gave him a grim smile. "It comes from years of practice. Anything you want to tell me?" She pinned him with her stare.

Dante almost blurted out that his engagement to Emma was a sham, but he bit down hard on his tongue to keep at least that little tidbit from her. The only two people who knew the truth were himself and Emma. No gossip would be able to pass it along to his mother. "No, Mother, I don't have anything else to tell you."

She snorted, her eyes narrowing slightly. "Well, get some sleep. I'll stay up with Sean for a while. I'm too wound up to sleep, anyway."

Dante ducked his head into his room. Emma was curled on her side, sound asleep, looking so small and fragile in his big bed. She didn't deserve to be hurt like she had. The fall could have broken every bone in her body or killed her.

She slept with her hand tucked beneath her cheek. She'd rolled up the sleeves of the big pajama shirt he never wore and looked even sexier in it than in a bikini.

Desire stirred inside him. Knowing he would do nothing to quench it that night, Dante slipped into the bathroom, stripped off his smelly clothes and turned on the cool water. After a quick scrub, he wrapped a towel around his waist, crossed the hallway and entered his room.

Normally he slept in the buff. To spare Emma some embarrassment, he slipped into the pajama bottoms that matched the top that she wore. He bent over her to check her breathing.

Emma rolled to her back and her eyes blinked open, two beautiful brown eyes that stared up at him sleepily. "Are you coming to bed?"

"I'll sleep on the couch."

"Please." She reached up and wrapped her arms around his neck, her lips soft and enticing.

He bent to brush his against them.

"Stay," she entreated, tightening her hold.

Knowing it would be difficult to lie in bed beside her and not touch her or make love to her, Dante heard himself agreeing before he'd thought it all the way through. "Okay, but just until you go back to sleep."

"No. All night." She scooted over, making room for his big body.

When he lay down beside her, she snuggled close, resting her head in the crook of his arm.

With a soft sigh, she closed her eyes and her breathing deepened.

Dante lay still for a long time, studying Emma in the light from the lamp on the nightstand.

Her dark hair lay in soft waves around her face, emphasizing her pale skin and the angry bruises.

She'd saved his life, only to put her own in danger. She didn't deserve it. Tomorrow, he'd get her out of there. Maybe the FBI had a safe house he could send her to until the trouble blew over.

And when they found the saboteur, he could resume his life as a CBP officer and maybe he'd look her up for a cup of coffee. If she dared see him again.

After all that had happened, he hadn't thought as much about Sam or the war that had taken her life. All his focus had gradually shifted to Emma.

Maybe it was time to let go of Sam and get on with his life.

Emma moaned in her sleep, her brow furrowing as if she were caught in a nightmare.

Dante gathered her close and pressed his lips to an uninjured spot. "It's okay," he whispered against her hair. "You're safe."

She settled against him and grew still, a smile tilting the corners of her lips.

Dante fell asleep with Emma in his arms, praying to the Great Spirit for her protection. He wasn't absolutely certain she was safe and that had him very concerned.

## Chapter Thirteen

Emma woke the next morning to sunlight pouring in through the window onto the bed, warming the blankets. Even before she opened her eyes, she reached out for the warm body beside her.

The spot next to her was empty, the sheets still warm. Dante hadn't been up long. The sheets still carried his scent and heat.

Emma rolled over onto her back and winced. Yes, she had some bumps and bruises, but it could have been so much worse.

Throwing back the covers, she eased out of the bed, her muscles sore and stiff. Someone had brought her bag into the room the night before. She rummaged for something to wear and unearthed a pretty red sweater and jeans.

Dressing quickly, she ran her brush through her hair and pulled it back, securing it with an elastic band. A quick peek out in the hallway and she padded across to the bathroom to relieve herself, wash her face and brush her teeth.

She left the bathroom and followed the sounds of voices down the hallway to the big kitchen where the Thunder Horse men sat around the table with their spouses.

Amelia stood by the stove, stirring fluffy yellow

scrambled eggs. "Sit, Emma. We were just talking about what happened yesterday and what the boys think we should do today. You might want to weigh in."

Roxanne sat beside Pierce, her dark red hair curling down around her shoulders, her arms crossed over her chest, green eyes flashing. "I'm not leaving. So you can get that thought right out of your mind, right now."

"Me, neither," Julia agreed. Lily ate slices of banana beside her in her high chair.

"Who's leaving?" Emma asked.

"Not us!" Amelia, Julia and Roxanne said as one.

Emma smiled. "I'm sorry, but I don't have a clue what you're talking about."

Dante stood and offered her his chair.

Pierce spoke up. "We were saying that it would be best for all the ladies to pack up and leave until we figure out who has been trying to hurt the Thunder Horse brothers." He tried to frown but winced for the effort.

Amelia scooped scrambled eggs onto a plate and set it on the table in front of Emma. "The men, bless their hearts, think they'd be doing us a favor by sending us off to the cities to shop until they can get to the bottom of the attacks on all of them."

Emma stared up at Dante. "Is that true?"

Dante's brows furrowed. "No. At least not the part about the shopping. However, we discussed it. After all that has happened, it's not safe for the women to be here."

Emma's eyes widened. "So you think we'll just pack up and leave because you men think that's the best thing for us?"

Dante's frown deepened. "Well, yes."

Emma fought the smile threatening to curl her lips. She liked seeing the consternation clearly written on

Dante's face and mirrored in Tuck's and Pierce's expressions. "Without giving any of us a choice?"

"It's the only way to keep you all safe," Dante said.

"Since I'm a guest here, I'll do whatever you say. But if I'm going to be booted out of the house, you should at least know my opinion of the ruling." She spoke quietly but with conviction that had the men listening. Heat rose up her cheeks as all gazes fixed on her. She crossed her arms and tilted her chin up. "I think it stinks."

The women all clapped their hands.

Roxanne took up the cause. "As Emma, the college professor, so eloquently put it, your idea stinks. So, get used to it. We're staying put until this storm blows over."

"And what if one of you gets hurt?" Pierce demanded. "Had that truck landed any other way, I'd be a dead man."

"We'll take our chances," Amelia said. "It's not for any one of you to make that decision for us. I can shoot just as well as any one of you boys. I know how to defend what is mine."

Emma let go of the smile that had been creeping up around the corners of her lips. She could just picture Amelia Thunder Horse wielding a rifle, loaded for bear. Her smile faded and she glanced up at Dante. "Again, I'm just a guest here. If you ask me to leave, I'll go back to my apartment in Grand Forks."

Dante's lips firmed. "No. Whoever shot down my helicopter knows you saw him. He might come after you in Grand Forks to eliminate any witnesses."

"That's the only other place I'd go."

"I'm still the head of this household." Amelia stood with her shoulders squared, holding her spatula like a scepter. "If Emma wants to stay, she can stay."

Emma smiled at the older woman, knowing that if Dante told her he wanted her to leave, she would. She was there because of him. As much as she appreciated Amelia's invitation, she wouldn't feel right staying if Dante wanted her gone.

The telephone hanging on the wall beside Tuck rang. He turned and answered it, walking out of the room with the cordless handset.

Dante pulled up a chair beside her. "You should eat. You missed dinner last night."

Emma lifted her fork, amazed at how hungry she was. She had a forkful of steaming eggs halfway to her mouth when Dante asked, "How are you feeling today?"

"I'm fine. A bit stiff and sore, but I'll live." She popped the eggs in her mouth and chewed.

"I wish you would let me take you to see the local doctor."

Emma swallowed. "Really, I'm okay." Then to end the argument, she shoved more eggs into her mouth. She wanted to be mad at his insistence on seeing a doctor, but it was nice for a change that someone was concerned about her health after her fall. Living so long on her own, she'd had to weather her illnesses alone.

Tuck returned to the kitchen and replaced the phone in its charger. "That was my buddy at the FBI. He ran that background check on Langley, Price and Ryan Yost." Tuck paused, frowning, his gaze going to his mother. "Price is clean of any criminal record. Langley had an assault on his record from a couple of years ago, but the woman who filed the complaint retracted it."

"The two of them showed up together on the property two weeks ago," Amelia said. "I told them then that I wasn't interested in discussing the sale of the land or the mineral rights."

"And they left?" Tuck asked.

"Yes." Amelia's brows dipped. "Then Monty Langley

came back the next day to ask if I'd consider leasing the mineral rights. He said he had some big oil company wanting to tap into the oil reserves beneath our property."

Roxanne nodded. "They hit me up for it, as well. I did some reading. As you're all aware, the oil industry is booming in North Dakota since they discovered the Bakken formation stretches from Canada all the way to Bismarck. This isn't the first time speculators have been to the ranch."

"Maddox handled them last summer," Amelia said. "Since Maddox has been gone, they might think they can coerce me into signing something."

Julia laughed. "They obviously don't know anything about you."

Amelia smiled, then said, "I need to talk to the lawyer and have each of my sons added as co-owners of the property. That way no one person—namely me—can sell without the permission of the other."

"I don't think any of us want the property sold or split up," Dante said. "This is our home. It wouldn't be right to break it up."

His mother pressed a hand to his shoulder. "Exactly."

Tuck cleared his throat. "Mom, you know how all of us brothers feel about Sheriff Yost."

"I know that you don't care for him." Her eyes narrowed. "Why?"

"It might be none of our business, but what is your relationship with the man?"

She looked away. "You know I've been going out to dinner with him. He's been a perfect gentleman with me."

Emma studied the looks on the Thunder Horse brothers' faces. Apparently they didn't trust the sheriff and found it troublesome that their mother did.

Amelia continued, "Though you're right, it's none of

your business who I date, I'm still young enough to appreciate being treated like a woman, not just someone's mother or grandmother." She smiled at Lily, who was happily smearing banana on her face.

When the men all stared at her as if she'd lost her marbles, Emma almost laughed. They only saw their mother.

Amelia Thunder Horse was still a beautiful woman with needs and desires of her own.

"Of course you're a woman," Tuck said. "And I have no problem with you dating. Dad's been gone for nearly three years now. You should get out and have some fun. Our concern is Yost. I had my buddy at the bureau run a check on Ryan Yost."

"He's the boy installing the security system in and around the house," she confirmed.

Tuck stared at his mother. "Do you trust him?"

Their mother's brows drew together. "I trust his father."

Pierce snorted a rude word beneath his breath.

Tuck continued, "Ryan had some scuffles with the law before he became of legal age and joined the military. After he served his time, he went back to Afghanistan as a civilian contractor for a couple of years."

"I know all that. He comes highly recommended by the security firm he works for." Amelia rested her hands on her hips. "I didn't hire him because he was William's son."

Tuck raised his hands. "Okay. I just want you to be cautious about the people you allow inside the house."

"I am. No one knows better than I do that a lone woman on a ranch out in the middle of nowhere is an easy target. Especially when Maddox is out of the country. That's why Maddox hired Sean. Having him here has been a godsend."

Sean nodded. "It's a pleasure to be here as protection for a beautiful woman who is nowhere past her prime."

All the Thunder Horse family stared at Sean in shock.

Sean held up his hands. "Just telling it like I see it. I'll shut up now." He leaned his back against the wall, a ruddy blush sneaking up beneath the tan on his cheeks.

Amelia's eyes flared and she glanced down, her lips curling. "Did you find anything else about Ryan Yost I should be concerned about?"

Tuck shook his head, almost as if he was disappointed. "Not yet."

Amelia lifted her head and stared at Tuck. "Then leave the boy alone. I want that system installed sometime in the near future." She folded a dishtowel over the handle of the oven and smoothed her blouse. "Now if you'll excuse me, I'd like to steal the ladies away from you." She raised her hand. "Not to take them on a shopping trip to the cities, but to help me sort through some things I want to box up and give to charity."

Emma finished her breakfast, washed her plate in the sink and left it to dry on the rack. She followed the sound of female voices to the last doorway at the end of the hallway. It opened into a large room with a massive bed positioned at the center of one wall and a fireplace in the corner with a cheery fire burning.

"We're in here," Julia called out.

Feeling like an outsider, Emma paused at the doorway into a large walk-in closet.

Amelia sat cross-legged on the floor in front of an old trunk filled with letters, photographs and scrapbooks. If not for the strands of gray hair among the darker ones, she could have been a woman half her age.

"You have to see these pictures." Julia patted the floor

beside her. "Look at Dante at five years old. Wasn't he a cutie?"

She handed Emma a picture of a little boy with dark hair hanging down to his shoulders.

"I let them wear their hair long during the summer. The boys liked pretending they were wild Indians in the Old West." Amelia chuckled. "They'd spend the summers shirtless and mostly barefoot, riding horses and helping their father as much as they could." She handed a photo to Julia. "This is Tuck when he was ten. All legs and skinny as a rail."

Julia laughed. "He was so thin."

Amelia reached for another stack of photos. "I couldn't keep meat on their bones. They ran it all off." She leafed through the pictures and handed them over to Roxanne. "There are so many of the boys hunting and fishing. We spent a lot of the summer camping out in the canyon. We'd count the wild ponies during the days and pick out the constellations in the stars at night."

Emma enjoyed hearing stories about the boys growing up on a ranch, spending their summers running around in the sun. She loved the outdoors. As a paleontologist she spent much of her time outside digging in the dirt. At night she'd lay out under the stars, dreaming about other people who'd lived long ago, staring up at the stars, just like she was.

Roxanne held out a photo. "Is this Pierce's father when he was young? Pierce looks just like him."

Emma leaned over at the same time as Julia and Amelia. The man in the picture looked much like Pierce, but he was standing with his arm around a young woman with midnight black hair, dark eyes and the high cheekbones of the Lakota.

"Yes, that's my John, before we met. He dated a young

woman from the reservation up until a week before we met. They had just broken up when he met me. I guess I caught him on the rebound." She tapped her finger to the picture. "She ended up marrying William Yost within a month of breaking up with John. She's Ryan Yost's mother. I believe her name was Mika, the Lakota name for *raccoon*."

Emma stared down at the woman with the dark eyes and sultry look. "She was pretty."

"I know." Amelia laughed. "I don't know what John saw in me."

"A beautiful woman with a big heart." Julia leaned over and hugged her mother-in-law. "I'm so glad I married into such a wonderful family."

Amelia kissed Julia's cheeks. "I love my sons, and I always wanted daughters. I couldn't have picked better ones than all of you."

Roxanne reached out to clasp Amelia's hand. "We love you."

Having just met the woman, Emma sat silent. She didn't feel as though she had the right to say anything, even if deep in her heart she knew the woman was genuinely good and loving. So she sat staring at the photo of the woman and Amelia's dead husband who looked very much like Dante.

How different would the family have been had John Thunder Horse married Mika?

And now Amelia had Mika's son working for her.

Amelia sighed. "How much of this stuff should I get rid of?"

Julia clasped the pile of photos to her chest. "None of the pictures."

"No, none of the photos." Amelia glanced at the clothing hanging above her head and stood. "I should give his clothes away. It isn't as if he'll need them anymore." She ran her hands along the rows of jeans and flannel shirts neatly hung by type and color. "He could wear overalls and look so handsome. I will always love John. But now that he's been gone for three years, it's time to let go of some of him to make room for the rest of my life."

"You're still so young. You deserve to find happiness." Julia stood and put her arm around Amelia.

"Is it wrong for me to think that way? Is it possible to find the love of your life twice in one lifetime?" Amelia laughed, her hand shifting to the opposite side of the closet. "For that matter, I should toss half of my clothes, as well. They remind me too much of my life with John. If I'm going to make a fresh start, I should start with a fresh wardrobe."

"That's the spirit." Roxanne fished a dress out off the rail. "Stay or throw?"

Amelia smiled. "I wore that the day John took me to Minneapolis to see *Cats* at the theater." She chuckled. "He hated sitting through all that singing, but he knew how much I loved it."

Roxanne's brows rose. "Does it stay or go?"

Amelia sucked in a deep breath and tilted her head sharply. "Go." She selected several more dresses and passed them to Julia, who set them on a chair outside the closet. Amelia made her way to the back of the closet and stopped, her hand freezing on a white garment bag hidden behind some old coats.

Roxanne reached over her head. "Let me." She unhooked the hanger from the rail and carried the garment bag out of the closet and laid it on the bed.

Emma followed her, wondering what was in the bag.

"With all my sons married or getting married, it brings back memories of my wedding to their father." Amelia emerged from the closet carrying a white hatbox slightly yellowed with age.

Julia perched on the edge of the bed beside the garment bag and made room for the hatbox. "How long did you know Tuck's father before you married?"

Amelia smiled. "Two weeks. He found me the last week of the *Medora Musical* in the Burning Hills Amphitheatre. I was one of the singers in the show. He stayed until all the guests had left and the cast was cleaning the theater afterward."

"I can't imagine John Thunder Horse sitting through the entire show." Roxanne's lips quirked upward. "I don't think I ever saw him when he wasn't riding a horse. He was always all about his horses and the ranch."

"Not that week. He asked me to marry him at the end of our first week together when I was supposed to head back to Bismarck where I was to start college that fall. I never went back to Bismarck to college. We eloped to Vegas a week later. He bought me this dress for our wedding in a little chapel on the strip." She unzipped the garment bag.

Inside was a timeless wedding dress made of soft, pearl-white satin. The V-shaped neckline was simple with a few lace and pearl embellishments. The back dropped low in an elegant scooped neckline. Understated and formfitting, the dress was perfect.

Emma's heart squeezed tight in her chest.

"I love this dress," Julia sighed. "I so wished it would have fit me when I married Tuck for the second time."

"I bet you were a beautiful bride." Roxanne ran her hand over the satin. "It's a gorgeous dress."

Amelia smiled at the gown. "I had hoped that one day my daughter would be able to wear my gown for her own wedding." The older woman chuckled.

"But you had four sons," Emma added, her own eyes misting. "Speaking as an only child, they were very lucky to have each other."

"Yes. My boys have had their differences, but for the most part, they would do anything for each other." Amelia lifted the dress out of the garment bag and held it up to Emma. "You and I are about the same height, and I was once about the same size as you, though you would never guess it now." She smiled up at Emma, her eyes shimmering with moisture. "I would be honored if you'd wear it for your wedding to Dante."

Emma held up her hands, horrified that this woman would offer this lovely dress to her when their engagement was fake. "I couldn't."

Amelia pulled the dress back. "Of course, you might have something altogether different in mind for your wedding. I'm sorry, I'm just a sentimental old fool."

Amelia looked anything but old, and Emma couldn't bear to break her heart. "No, I think the dress is absolutely perfect in every way. It's just…" What could she say? That she'd lied all along, that she never intended to marry her son? "It's just that I hadn't even thought that far ahead." She gave Dante's mother a weak smile. "But when I do marry, that dress would be exactly the kind of dress I'd always dreamed of."

"Try it on," Julia insisted. "We want to see you in it, don't we, Roxanne?"

"You bet." Roxanne sat on the edge of the bed. "Go on. If you're embarrassed about changing in front of us, you can go into the closet and close the door. It's big enough for an army to change in."

Before she could protest, Amelia laid the dress across her arms and turned her toward the closet door. "Do you need help getting into it?"

"No, I can manage." Emma needed help getting out of the big fat lie she'd told. With the three women waiting in the bedroom for her to come out in the wedding dress, Emma had no choice. She stripped out of her jeans and the sweater she'd put on that morning, unhooked her bra and stepped into the gown.

The satin slipped across her skin, light and smooth, gliding over her hips so easily it felt like air. She reached behind her and zipped the back, a little apprehensive about how low the neckline dipped down her back, almost to her waist.

The dress could have been tailored for her; it fit perfectly, hugging her hips and breasts like a second skin. The skirt fell in an A-line, pooling at her feet, the train stretching out three feet behind her. A full-length mirror hung on the back of the door. When Emma looked up and caught a glimpse of her reflection, she gasped and froze, tears welling in her eyes.

It was absolutely exquisite.

"Come out, we want to see!" Julia called.

Hating herself for the lie she was perpetuating, Emma opened the door and stepped out of the closet.

The women had been talking, but when they spotted her standing there, the room grew so silent Emma could hear the crackle of the fire in the fireplace.

Amelia covered her mouth with her hands and tears slipped down her cheeks. "Emma," she said, her voice cracking.

"You're beautiful," Julia said, her voice barely a whisper.

"Wait." Amelia opened the hatbox and pulled out a bridal veil, unfolding the lengths of lace-trimmed tulle. She pressed the comb into Emma's hair and turned her toward a full-length mirror.

The woman staring back at her was a stranger. Dressed as a bride, her hair around her shoulders, the veil framing her pale face, she wanted to cry.

"I'm no expert, but I think you found your dress," Roxanne announced, clapping her hands together. "It couldn't be more perfect if you'd had it designed for you."

Amelia reached for Emma and hugged her. "Dante is a very lucky man to have found you."

What could Emma say to that? Nothing. He hadn't actually found her. She'd found him dragging himself out of his burning aircraft.

"Do you like it?" Amelia held her at arm's length, her gaze searching Emma's face. "You can tell me if you don't. I won't be offended."

Emma glanced down at the satin dress and nodded. "I love it." Feeling more of a heel by the minute, Emma backed out of Amelia's arms. "I'm sorry. But I think the fall yesterday took its toll on me. If you don't mind, I need to go lie down."

Amelia's eyes widened. "Of course, dear. How inconsiderate of me. I should have known better than to keep you rummaging through my closets. Here, let me unzip you." She helped unzip the dress and Emma ran for the closet where she removed the veil, stripped out of the beautiful dress and put her own clothes back on.

When she was finished, she emerged from the closet. The women were busy folding the clothes that would go to charity. Emma laid the veil and dress on the bed, her fingers skimming across the smooth satin fabric, regret tugging at her.

"Please excuse me," she said and hurried from the room.

She ran for the bedroom she and Dante had slept in the night before and crawled up in the bed, pulling the blanket around her. It still smelled of Dante. As she lay there, she thought of Dante helping her out of the collapsing trailer first, when it meant he might not make it out at all. She thought of how he'd helped an injured horse out of the canyon in the frigid cold, of how he'd risked his life rather than leave her in the canyon any longer than he had to.

She still tingled all over when she thought of the way it felt when Dante wrapped her in his arms, and how gentle he'd been when they'd made love for her first time, and then again in her apartment. She remembered their first kiss and the way it felt to lie in bed beside him.

Then she thought of how beautiful she felt in his mother's wedding dress and of the lies she'd told these good people. Of how they'd hate her when they learned the truth.

Tears slid down her cheeks as she realized what had happened in the short amount of time she'd been with Dante. No matter how much she'd told herself not to get involved, she'd done it. She'd fallen head over heels in love with the big Lakota man.

And no matter how much she might love him, Dante was in love with a dead woman and had told her up front he wasn't looking for a relationship. He wasn't ready.

Her chest hollow, Emma curled into a ball, buried her face in the pillow and cried.

When she could cry no more, she promised herself to leave at the first opportunity. She couldn't stay there, in love with Dante and his family, when it would all end. The sooner she severed the ties, the sooner she could start getting over him.

## Chapter Fourteen

Dante, Pierce, Tuck and Sean fed the horses and worked with Sweet Jessie's sore foot. The swelling was down and the horse was impatient to be outside. They all agreed it would be better to keep her in the warm, dry barn until the wound had scabbed over a bit.

Dante gave the horse sweet feed and water and ran a currycomb over her fuzzy coat.

When he and his brothers stepped out of the barn, they noticed a vehicle pulling up in front of the house. After all that had happened, Dante wasn't comfortable with anyone driving up to the ranch house that didn't have an appointment or who hadn't called first. He hurried to the house, bursting through the kitchen door.

Following the voices, he found his mother, Roxanne and Julia in the front foyer, talking to a young man with jet-black hair and dark skin, about Dante's own age.

Julia turned to Dante. "You remember Ryan Yost, don't you?"

Dante nodded. "We spoke yesterday."

Ryan shifted the box he carried from one hand to the other and held out his hand. "Dante."

Dante shook his hand. "Ryan."

The other man held up a box. "Those cameras came in like I thought they would."

Amelia waved him inside. "Let me know if you need anything."

"Thank you, ma'am. I think I have all that I need, except a ladder."

"I'll get it," Sean offered and headed for the back door. Moments later, he came in dusting snow off his jacket and carrying a ladder.

Dante watched as Ryan set the ladder up in the living room, attach a camera to the wires in the corner and screw the mount into the wall.

Tuck joined Dante at the edge of the room. "I think Sean and Pierce can handle things here. Why don't you and I go to Medora and question the oil speculators?"

Dante nodded. "Let me check in on Emma."

His mother stopped him in the hallway. "Don't forget tonight is the kickoff of the Cowboy Christmas events in Medora. It's a tradition for the family to attend. I'd like to take Emma, as well."

"She'd like that." Dante smiled. "Tuck and I can meet you in town so you don't have to wait on us."

His mother nodded. "That's a good idea."

Dante stepped into the room where Emma lay sleeping, the blankets pulled up around her. He tiptoed to the bed and stared down at her face. Her dark hair splayed across the white pillowcase and her cheeks appeared to be streaked with tears.

Why would she be crying? Were her injuries more than she was letting on? Did she miss her home in Grand Forks?

His chest tightened. He found himself wanting to take away her pain. Dante brushed the hair from her face and bent to kiss her cheek.

Emma turned her face at the last minute and their lips

brushed together. Her arm slid up around his neck, dragging him closer.

"I'm heading to town to question the speculators. Will you meet me at the diner later when the family comes to town for the festival?"

"Mmm."

He kissed her again, this time, deepening the kiss, his tongue sliding between her teeth to caress hers.

She returned the pressure, her response stronger this time.

When he reluctantly broke away, she looked up at him with dark brown eyes, the shadows beneath them making her appear sad. "Be careful," she said.

"You, too." He brushed his knuckles against the softness of her face. "I'll see you later."

"Goodbye," she whispered.

Dante left the room, feeling as though he should stay and spend the afternoon holding Emma. He hadn't thought much about Sam since Emma had come into his life. Even the guilt he'd experienced at first was fading. He finally realized Sam would have wanted him to get on with his life.

With Emma he could see a future.

His mother followed him to the front door where he dressed for the outdoors and waited for his brother to appear.

"You know she's special, don't you?" his mother said as she held his coat for him while he slipped his arms into the sleeves.

"Who, Emma?" He chuckled. "Yeah. I know."

"Then don't let her get away."

He paused and stared down at his mother. "Why would I?"

She snorted softly, holding on to his gloves. "How

many times have you successfully lied to me, Dante Thunder Horse?" she demanded.

He thought back over the years and his lips twisted. "Never."

"That's right." She handed the gloves over. "I knew when you made the announcement at the hospital that you were lying."

"I'm sorry, Mom. I shouldn't have. But I didn't want to worry you more with Pierce lying in ICU."

"Actually, I'm glad you did. It gave *you* time to get to know her better and to see how much you really care about her."

"Mom, I've only known her a few days. That's not enough to base a lifetime of marriage on."

His mother shook her head. "That's all it took for me and your father. We knew within the first hour of talking. He proposed after a week and we were married for thirty years before he passed."

"I didn't think I could love again."

"Sam was a different chapter in your life. Emma is a fresh beginning."

"I'll always love Sam."

"Son, that's the beauty of the human heart. You don't have to stop loving Sam, just like I'll never stop loving your father. But there is someone else out there you could love, as well. And I'm hoping that there might be someone out there for me. I'm not too old to want someone else in my life. I have you boys, but you have your own families."

He squeezed her hand gently. "And you deserve to love again."

"As do you."

Dante pulled his mother into his arms and hugged her. "Please tell me you're not considering Sheriff Yost."

She laughed. "I had, but I'm not so sure anymore. I think I'll keep my options open."

Sean appeared from the direction of the kitchen. "I put a pot of coffee on, care to join me?"

Amelia smiled up at Dante. "I do have options, you know."

Dante grinned as his mother left him to join Sean for that cup of coffee in the kitchen.

"Ready?" Tuck asked as he pushed past him to exit out the front door. "We're going in my truck. And we'd better hurry if we want to talk to the oil speculators before the town gets crowded for the Cowboy Christmas kickoff."

Dante almost told Tuck he'd question the men tomorrow. He wanted to go back into the room with Emma, pull her into his arms and tell her…

Tell her what?

That he could be well on his way to falling in love with her and would she give him a chance to find out?

With the idea too new to him, he decided he'd be better off waiting until later that night to hold her in his arms and make it right.

EMMA MUST HAVE fallen back asleep after Dante left. She didn't wake until Amelia poked her head in the doorway a couple of hours later.

"Emma, it's time to get ready. We're all heading into Medora for the kickoff of the annual Cowboy Christmas festivities. We leave in thirty minutes."

"I'm awake," she assured the woman. She sat up, feeling every bruise and bump and stiff muscle in her body, along with the deep sadness of knowing she'd be leaving. On the nightstand beside a glass of water, lay the keys to the SUV Dante had rented in Grand Forks.

If she really was leaving, now would be the best time

to do it. With Dante in town, the rest of the members of his household leaving for Medora, she could sneak away. She slipped into her snow gear and pulled on her boots.

Stuffing her toothbrush, hairbrush and a change of clothes in her purse, she left the rest of the contents of her bag in the bedroom and stepped out in the hallway.

"Look at you, all ready to go," Julia said, hurrying to one of the bedrooms. "We'll be a few more minutes. We had to wait for Ryan to leave before we could begin getting ready."

"He was here?"

"While you were asleep. Got half of the cameras wired. He's supposed to be back tomorrow to finish the job."

"I didn't even hear him working," Emma said.

"We had him work on the installation of the cameras at the other end of the house so that he wouldn't disturb you and Lily while you both napped." A tiny cry came from down the hallway. "That's my cue. All I have to do is get Lily dressed and I'll be ready."

Amelia emerged from her bedroom, wearing a bright red Christmas sweater. "I had a call from Maddox while you were sleeping. He and Katya flew into Bismarck over an hour ago. They're on their way and should be to Medora in time for the festivities. Isn't that wonderful?" The older woman beamed. "All my children home for Christmas." She wrapped her arms around Emma and hugged her tight. "I'm so glad you're here with us."

Guilt tugged at Emma as she returned the hug. "Thank you for all you've done for me," she said, fighting back tears. "I'm supposed to meet Dante at the diner. Do you mind if I leave a little early? I have a few things I want to pick up at the store before it closes."

Amelia's brows furrowed. "Is that a good idea to go off on your own with all that's happened?"

Emma forced a smile to her stiff lips. "I'll be fine. If I have any trouble on the road, all of you will be behind me shortly. I'll just wait until you come along."

"I could be ready to go in five minutes," Amelia assured her. "Just let me touch up my makeup and grab my purse."

"No hurry. I really can manage this on my own." Emma hugged Amelia one more time. "Goodbye." Before Amelia could come up with another argument to keep her there or go with her, Emma hurried out the door to the SUV and climbed in.

The vehicle started right up, of course. It couldn't be cranky and die to keep her from making her break from the Thunder Horses. Deep down, she wanted to stay and become a part of this family. But she couldn't make Dante love her and she wouldn't stay knowing he didn't and never would.

The stolen kisses and making love had only been a passing fancy to him. His heart would always belong to Sam.

Shifting into Reverse, she backed up, turned and drove down the long driveway toward the highway. She took one last glance in her rearview mirror before the ranch house blended into the snow and all she could see was the thin wisp of smoke from the fireplace.

She turned onto the highway headed toward Medora and the interstate highway that would take her back east. She could stop in Bismarck and stay the night or push through and arrive in Grand Forks around midnight.

Snow fell in big, fluffy flakes, thickening the farther she drove from the Thunder Horse Ranch, making it difficult to see the road in front of her. As she came to a crossroad with a stop sign, she pressed her foot to the brake.

The tires skidded and she started sliding toward the ditch.

Heart pumping, she turned into the skid and righted the vehicle, just in time to see the form of a man walking alongside the road ahead, headed toward her.

As her lights caught him in their beams, he lifted his head and waved her down.

Carefully applying her breaks, she slowed and rolled down the passenger window.

"Thank goodness you stopped." Ryan Yost poked his head through the window. "I thought I'd have to walk all the way back to the ranch house."

"What happened to your truck?" Emma asked.

"It slid into the ditch about half a mile ahead. The roads are pretty tricky."

"Are you headed back to the ranch or to town?"

"To Medora, if you don't mind."

She popped the locks on the SUV and the man climbed into the passenger seat.

"Where is the rest of the Thunder Horse clan?"

"They should be right behind me."

"In that case, turn here," Ryan said.

"What?" Emma glanced at the dirt track leading off the road. "Why?"

"Because I said so." Ryan grabbed the steering wheel and yanked it to the right.

Emma held on as the SUV bumped off the road onto the narrow strip of dirt lightly covered in snow. Pulse pounding, she fought to right the vehicle. When she had the SUV under control, she braked to a stop and shot an angry glance at Ryan. "What the hell are you doing?"

That's when she saw the dark, hard form of the gun

in his hand pointed at her head, and a rush of icy-cold dread washed over her.

"I'm taking what should have been mine."

Knowing she could be a victim or she could try to escape, Emma chose to try rather than go along with whatever Ryan had in mind. "Why do you say that? What should have been yours? Surely not me." She spoke calmly while her left hand inched toward the door handle.

Ryan laughed. "It's not you, but I've learned that to get to them, you have to go through the ones they love."

"Are you talking about the Thunder Horses?" she asked.

"Of course I'm talking about the Thunder Horses. Keep driving," he commanded. "Far enough off the road they won't see you when they drive by."

Emma eased her foot off the brake but didn't apply her foot to the accelerator. The vehicle inched forward along the bumpy road.

"Faster!" Ryan yelled and leaned across to slam his own foot down on hers. The vehicle leaped forward.

At that moment, Emma flung the door open, elbowed the man in the face and threw herself out of the vehicle. She hit the rocky ground hard and rolled out of the way of the tires.

Pain shot through the arm she'd landed on, but she scrambled to her feet and ran as fast as she could in the snow and her clunky boots.

A car door slammed and gravel crunched behind her.

By the time she reached the paved road, her lungs burned from breathing the frigid air and her muscles were screaming, but she pushed forward. Her foot hit the icy surface and she skidded and slammed onto the pavement flat on her back, the wind knocked out of her lungs.

Lights blinked far down the road toward the ranch

house. If only she could get up and keep running. They'd find her.

Emma sucked in a breath, rolled over onto her hands and knees and tried to get up.

Ryan hit her like a linebacker, plowing into her and knocking her into the ditch on the other side of the road. He landed on top of her and covered her with his body, pressing her face into the snow and ice.

She struggled, but he weighed more than she did and he had her arms and legs pinned beneath his.

The muffled sound of a vehicle engine came and went. Though she tried to scream out, she knew she wouldn't be heard. Even if she was, he might still have his gun on him. What would happen if they stopped? Would he shoot Amelia, Julia or Lily before the men took him down?

Emma wouldn't be able to live with herself if he did, so she lay quietly, no longer fighting to free herself. Once the vehicle drove by, she'd come up with another plan. If she lived long enough.

## Chapter Fifteen

Dante and Tuck stopped at the hotel where the oil speculators were staying. Nicole was on duty, looking as bored as usual. "Ah, the Thunder Horse brothers. Here to see Ryan, again?"

"We're not here to see Ryan. We'd like to talk with Monty Langley and Theron Price."

"Sorry, unless you have an appointment, they've asked not to be disturbed."

Tuck pulled out his FBI credentials. "What room are they in?"

Nicole stared at the big *F-B-I* letters and nodded. "Impressive." She jerked her head toward the hallway. "They have rooms 109 and 110."

As Tuck and Dante took off in that direction, she called out, "But they aren't there."

"Any idea where they are?"

"Why do you want to know?"

"I can't answer that."

"They just got back from a ride on their snowmobiles." She snorted. "They usually have dinner at the diner around this time every day, like clockwork. I'd check there."

"They own snowmobiles?" Dante asked.

"Yeah, they keep them out back in the storage shed."

"How do we get inside the shed?"

Nicole shrugged. "Open it. We don't lock it."

Dante left the hotel and ran around the outside to the back where a weathered storage shed stood in the corner of the lot. He pushed the door open and stepped inside. The light from the doorway splashed across two fairly new snowmobiles.

"So, they own snowmobiles," Tuck said. "So do most of the people in this area."

"The one that was out by the canyon had a broken track and was leaking oil." He studied the one closest to him while Tuck dropped to his haunches beside the other.

After a moment, Tuck straightened. "This one doesn't have a broken track or an oil leakage."

The lighting wasn't the best, so Dante skimmed his hand along the top of the vehicle closest to him, feeling the tracks for any inconsistencies. One of the tracks had a notch chipped out of it. Ducking his head, Dante saw something shiny on the ground beneath the engine. He reached his hand beneath it and felt warm, sticky oil.

"A lot of snowmobiles have chinks out of their tracks and leak oil."

"Yeah, but I don't believe in coincidence." Dante left the storage shed.

"Where to?" Tuck asked.

"The diner, to find us some oil speculators."

He and Tuck climbed in the truck and drove the block to the diner, parking in front.

Through the windows Dante could see Hank and Florence at the bar counter. At a table on the south side of the diner, two men sat drinking coffee.

Dante was first out of the truck and into the diner. He marched up to the two men. "Monty Langley and Theron Price?"

The younger one with sandy-blond hair raised his eyebrows. "I'm Monty, he's Theron. What can we do for you?"

"Where were you two yesterday around three o'clock in the afternoon?"

"Why?" Monty asked.

Tuck stepped up beside Dante and flashed his FBI badge. "Just answer the question."

Monty raised his hands. "We were here in the diner with Mr. Plessinger for most of the afternoon. About have him ready to lease his mineral rights." He dropped his arms and smiled. "Are you two ready to talk money?"

"Hell no," Dante responded.

Theron frowned. "Then what's this all about?"

"Someone tried to kill me and my fiancée yesterday out at the canyon. He used C-4 explosives. The kind people might have access to if connected with an oil drilling operation."

Monty stood, his hands raised. "Whoa there, cowboy. I'm a lover, not a killer. The closest I get to the oil is when I take my car in for an oil change."

Florence stepped into the conversation. "I can vouch for the two of them. They worked over poor ol' Fred Plessinger all afternoon, drank two pots of coffee between them and ate an entire coconut cream pie."

Tuck's cell phone buzzed and he stepped away from the group to answer it.

"Where were you two four days ago? Were you anywhere near Grand Forks?"

"We've been here in Medora the entire week," Price said. "We're not scheduled to head back to Minneapolis until the end of the month."

"Do you have proof?" Dante asked.

Monty pulled a pocket-size day planner out of his

jacket and handed it to Dante. "Look at my schedule. Any one of these people I've had appointments with can vouch for my whereabouts."

Dante glanced at the names on the man's minicalendar. He recognized many of them. The men seemed slimy but legit in their alibis. He handed the planner to Monty. "I'm sorry to have bothered you."

"Sounds like someone is out to get the Thunder Horse clan. What with your brothers' brakes going out, your helicopter going down and now the explosives. Do you all have good insurance policies?" Monty held out a card. "I have a friend who sells life insurance."

Dante walked away and joined Tuck near the door.

"Are you sure?" Tuck ran a hand through his hair, his face pale. "Thanks. I'm on it." As soon as Tuck hung up, he pushed through the door. "Come on, we have to go."

"What's wrong?"

Tuck climbed into his truck and started the engine as Dante slid into the passenger seat. "I had my contact at the FBI run a check on flight plans for Grand Forks and Bismarck to see if Ryan Yost's name or plane came up. They had a couple of hits. He flew into Bismarck two days before your crash and out the next day, landing in Grand Forks the day before your crash. Then he flew out of Grand Forks a couple of days after your crash."

Dante's blood ran cold. "It adds up all too well. He could have cut your brakes and left them to bleed out, hopped in his plane to Grand Forks to target me. Now he's out at the house with the family."

"Pierce and Sean are there," Tuck said, pulling out of the diner parking lot onto the highway.

"But they're not suspecting anything." Dante hit the speed-dial number for home and pressed his cell phone to his ear. It rang five times before he gave up. "No answer."

"They could be on their way to town for Cowboy Christmas." Tuck glanced ahead as they approached the edge of town. "As a matter of fact, isn't that Pierce's SUV?"

The SUV pulled up beside them, the window rolled down and Pierce stuck his head out. "You're headed the wrong way."

"Where's Ryan Yost?"

"He left thirty minutes before us. I figure he's back at his hotel," Pierce said. "Why?"

"Do you have everyone with you?"

His mother answered, "Yes, we do. Except Emma. She was on her way to meet you at the diner." She unbuckled her seat belt and leaned over Pierce's shoulder. "Emma's not with you? She left ten minutes before we did."

Dante's heart fell down around his knees. Emma was missing and Ryan Yost might be the one responsible. Where would he take her? And why?

His cell phone buzzed in his hand and he glanced down. A text message came through with a number he didn't recognize in the display screen.

If you want to see Emma alive, come to the ranch. Alone.

Dante's hand shook as he held out the phone to Tuck.

Tuck read the message and glanced over at Pierce. "We have a problem."

Pierce pulled off the road, climbed out of the SUV and walked over to Tuck's truck. The three brothers read the message again.

"He's at the ranch with Emma," Dante said. "I have to go."

"Who's at the ranch with Emma?" Pierce asked.

"Ryan Yost."

"Where's Emma?" Dante's mother pushed her way through her sons. "And why are you concerned about Ryan?"

Dante debated telling her something to pacify her, but the look on her face was enough. "We think Ryan Yost has her. I just got this text." He showed his mother the cell phone.

"Oh, dear Lord. I knew I should have insisted she ride with us."

"If she had, you all might be the ones he's holding hostage."

Amelia stared up at her sons. "But why?"

"Good question. Only Ryan can answer that. For now, I have to go." Dante held out his hands to his brother Tuck. "Give me the keys."

"You're not going alone."

"I have to. If I don't, he might kill Emma."

"He might kill her anyway. Why not let us come with you? We're the ones trained for this."

"You forget I fought in the war."

"Yeah, but you have no training in hostage negotiation."

"I can't risk it." Dante climbed into the truck and stuck the key in the ignition.

"We're coming with you." Pierce opened the back door and got in the crew cab.

Tuck climbed into the passenger seat. "What he doesn't know won't hurt. We have your back."

"What about me?" Amelia asked.

"Maddox is supposed to arrive about now. Send him out when he does. And, Mom, I need you to stay in town and keep Lily and Julia safe," Tuck said. "Promise me."

Amelia nodded. "And promise me that you three won't do anything stupid and get yourselves shot."

"We promise," they said as one.

"Want me to notify the sheriff's department?" she asked.

"No!" they said in unison. "If it's his son, he might take sides. The wrong side."

"Got it." Amelia stepped away from the truck and raised her hand. *"Wakan tanan kici un wakina chelee."*

Dante drove toward the ranch, his foot heavy on the accelerator. He appreciated his mother's prayer to the Great Spirit, but he wasn't the one who needed it.

Emma was.

## Chapter Sixteen

Emma came to and blinked at the lights shining from the lamps on end tables above her. For a moment she was disoriented, her vision blurred and pain throbbed at her temple.

The last thing she remembered was fighting to stand after the SUV full of the Thunder Horse family had passed by. One moment she'd gotten a good kick at his shins, the next moment she was awake in the living room of the Thunder Horse ranch house.

"Looks like you'll be around for the fireworks after all," a voice said.

She turned her head, a flash of pain making her close her eyes until it passed. When she opened them again, she could see Ryan Yost standing beside the window, peering through a crack in the blinds.

"Someone's coming. Let's hope it's the people I specifically requested and not any more." He clapped his hands together. "Today, I finally get my revenge on the people I hate the most."

Emma struggled to push to a sitting position, realizing that her hands were secured behind her back by something that felt like duct tape. Using her elbow, she pushed up and drew her legs under her, sitting up. Thankfully, he hadn't tied her feet together. She glanced around for something sharp to rub the tape on. Every edge seemed to be soft or rounded. "Why are you doing this?"

"I'll tell you why. For years, my father hated me, hated my mother and hated everything about our lives together. When my mother couldn't take it any longer, she jerked me out of my school here in Medora and hauled me back to the reservation where I would have rotted in hell."

Emma's head ached, but she had to keep the man talking. Maybe she could reason with him. "And what does that have to do with the Thunder Horses?"

"On one of her normal drunken binges, she let slip a secret she'd kept from me and from my father. A secret that made everything perfectly clear. William Yost was in love with the woman who married John Thunder Horse, not my mother."

"So?"

"And my mother was in love with John Thunder Horse and they'd been dating up until John met Amelia and dumped my mother. My pregnant mother."

Emma's mind cleared and focused on what the man had just said. "Are you saying John Thunder Horse was your father?"

"Damn right he was. He left my mother when she was pregnant. She was forced to marry Yost and had me eight months later."

Ryan slapped a hand to his chest. "I should have grown up on the Thunder Horse Ranch, not that hellhole of a reservation. I should have had the best of everything they had."

"Are you certain? Have you done a DNA test?"

"I look like a Thunder Horse, damn it!" He jerked Emma up by her arm and glared into her face. "I've never looked anything like William Yost."

"Because you look like your mother." Sheriff Yost

stepped into the house, gun drawn, closing the door behind him. "Ryan, what are you doing?"

"Daddy." Ryan practically spit the word out. "So glad you could come to your *son's* coming out party. Pull up a seat. We're waiting for the other main player to arrive."

Footsteps pounded on the porch outside and a voice shouted, "Emma!"

"Dante, don't come in!" Emma cried.

Ryan looped his arm around her neck and yanked her up by the throat. "Shut up."

Dante flung the door open and entered, his eyes blazing. "Leave her out of this, Ryan."

"Oh, no. I wouldn't dream of it. I've worked too hard setting this all up to end it here."

"What do you want? The ranch? Money? You name it." Dante stepped closer.

"Stop right there." Ryan pointed his gun at Emma's temple. "Another step closer and I'll shoot her."

"Why are you doing this, son?"

"Because I'm not your son."

"What are you talking about?"

"My mother told me her secret. A secret I suspect you always knew. She had an affair with John Thunder Horse before she married you, and before *he* married Amelia. She was pregnant when you married her. That's why I was born eight months after your wedding."

Sheriff Yost raised a hand. "Whoa, son, where did you hear such an idiotic story?"

"From my mother. The woman you kicked out of your house and sent back to live on the reservation. If I had been your son, you wouldn't have let her take me." Ryan's lip curled back, baring his teeth. "It all made sense when she told me I was John Thunder Horse's son. You hated me, and you hated my mother for what she did."

Ryan's arm tightened around Emma's neck. She struggled, unable to get air past her vocal cords to utter a protest.

"Let go of Emma," Dante pleaded. Emma's face was beet-red and starting to turn blue. "She had nothing to do with what happened between your father and mother."

"No way. While you and your brothers lived the life *I* should have, I wallowed in a broken-down trailer while my mother drank herself into oblivion every night. When she wasn't slapping me around, she was telling me what a failure I was compared to the four of you."

"Ryan, I don't know what your mother told you, but it was a pack of lies. I tried to get you back, but the court didn't want to go up against the tribal council. Your mother told them she wanted you to grow up knowing the way of your ancestors. They wouldn't listen to me. I loved you. I wanted you to live with me."

"Then why did you kick us out?"

"I didn't." Yost stepped closer. "You have to believe me. Your mother had problems. She was delusional. I think her breakup with John was the last straw. I didn't see it until we'd already married. And with you on the way, I couldn't divorce her."

"Lies!" Ryan dragged Emma back toward the hallway. "You threw us out."

"She told you that, didn't she?" William said quietly. "The truth was that she left me and took you with her to punish me."

"No. That's not how it was. You hated me and ruined my life. Now I'm going to ruin yours." Ryan's hand shook as he held it to Emma's head. "If you don't shoot Dante right now, I'll put a bullet through Emma's head."

"What will shooting Dante gain for you?"

"It'll be one Thunder Horse down and you will have

killed him. Amelia will never love you after you've killed her precious son." Ryan's face turned red, his eyes bulging. "Shoot him now or I swear the woman dies!"

Dante turned to the sheriff. "Do it. Shoot me if that's what it'll take to free Emma. She'll die anyway if he doesn't loosen his hold soon."

"I can't shoot you." The sheriff held his gun to the side. "I won't."

"I've never trusted you. Never thought you were man enough to fill my father's shoes or deserve to be with my mother. If ever there's a time to prove me wrong, now is it. Shoot me." Dante held his arms out to his sides, glancing over at Emma's face turning purple. "Now!" He prayed Yost would do it, but that he'd graze him, not hit him in a place that would be fatal. If Ryan thought him dead, he might let go of Emma long enough for her to breathe, buying time.

Sheriff Yost raised his 9 mm pistol and aimed. "God have mercy on my soul." He pulled the trigger.

The bullet's impact jerked Dante's arm back and he was flung to the side, angling toward Ryan Yost.

As Dante crashed to the floor, Ryan loosened his hold on Emma's neck.

Her knees buckled and she slipped to the floor.

Ryan raised his gun, pointing it at Sheriff Yost. "Now I'll be the hero for shooting the man who killed Amelia's son, and you will be blamed for setting off the explosives I have positioned around the house." Before he could pull the trigger, Dante swung his leg, sweeping Ryan's feet out from under him. His shot hit the ceiling and he landed hard on his back, his gun skidding across the hardwood floor out of his reach.

Emma, having caught her breath, spun around on her hip and kicked the gun farther away from him.

"No! You'll ruin everything." Ryan grabbed her hair and yanked hard.

Dante, his arm bleeding and his vision getting gray and fuzzy around the edges, flung himself on top of Ryan, pinning him down with his good hand, keeping him from digging the detonator out of his pocket.

Then everything seemed to happen at once. Tuck and Pierce stormed into the house, followed by Maddox and the rest of the family.

Tuck pulled Dante off Ryan.

"Don't let him get his hands in his pockets. He has a detonator in it and he says he has the house rigged to explode."

Tuck rolled Ryan onto his belly and slapped a zip tie around his wrists, then carefully dug the detonation device from his pocket and set it aside for the bomb squad. "You have the right to remain silent…"

As Tuck read Ryan his Miranda rights, Dante crawled over to where Emma was struggling to get up with her wrists still bound behind her back with duct tape.

Maddox leaned over Dante. "Let me get her." He pulled a pocketknife out of his pocket and sliced through the tape, freeing her wrists.

As soon as she was free, Emma flung her arms around Dante's shoulders. "I thought you were dead. Why the hell did you tell the sheriff to shoot you?"

"Sweetheart, you were turning a pretty shade of blueberry. Another minute and you wouldn't have made it." He winced, pain slicing through him where she hugged his injured arm. "I'm getting blood on your clothes."

"Oh, my God. Lie down. Someone call an ambulance."

Pierce handed her a towel. "Apply pressure to the wound to slow the bleeding."

Tuck placed a call to 9-1-1, requesting an ambulance and bomb-sniffing dogs.

While Maddox helped Dante out of his jacket, Emma folded the hand towel into a wad. Once Dante was out of the jacket, the wound bled freely. Emma eased Dante onto his back and applied pressure to the wound.

"Emma." Dante grasped the wrist holding the towel in place.

"Am I hurting you?"

"More than you'll ever know."

"I'm sorry, but if I let up, you'll start bleeding again."

He chuckled. "Not the arm." He laid his other hand over her chest. "Here. You're hurting my heart."

"I don't understand."

"You made me feel again." He lifted her empty hand and pressed it to his chest. "You made me ache so bad I thought I was going to die."

Her eyes misted. "I'm sorry, I don't want to cause you any pain. I know how much you loved Sam. I was leaving to go back to Grand Forks so that I wouldn't make you feel like you had to choose."

"That's the point. I didn't want to love anyone else. I didn't want to choose between you and her. But then you ran your snowmobile into a man who tried to kill me not once but three times.

"I'd have done it for anyone."

"I know. That's what I love about you. You're selfless, endearing and beautiful in so many ways."

"No, I'm just me. A college professor with very few social skills."

"You have all the skills I need, and you're the most beautiful woman I know. Because you're beautiful inside and out. You showed me that I didn't have to choose. That I could love you both."

Emma laughed, the sound catching on a sob. "You've been talking to your mother, haven't you?"

"She's smarter than I ever gave her credit for." Dante pressed her hand to his lips kissing her knuckles. "I'll never underestimate her again. Nor you."

As Tuck dragged Ryan to his feet and shoved him toward the door, the rest of the Thunder Horse family arrived with the ambulance, a state policeman and the only other deputy on duty in Billings County. Rather than risk anyone else being hurt, the party was moved out of the house.

Ryan was bundled into the state police car and carted off to Bismarck where he would face a multitude of charges.

Sheriff Yost hung around to make sure no one went inside the house his son had rigged with explosives.

Dante let the medics bandage his wound but refused to go with them to the hospital in Dickinson. "I want to make sure my fiancée doesn't run out on me." He held on to Emma's hand as he sat on the gurney, his legs dangling over the side.

Emma smiled sadly. "But don't you see? It's over. You don't have to protect me anymore. I can go back to Grand Forks."

"Is that what you want?" he asked.

Her head dipped and she stared at her feet, which were up to her ankles in snow. "You said no guarantees."

"Yeah, well, I was wrong."

His mother walked up to him where he sat and laid a hand on his shoulder. "Dante."

"Just a minute, Mother."

"No, really, if you want to do this right, take this." She removed the glove from his hand and one of hers. Then she slipped the diamond engagement ring off her finger.

The ring his father had given her when he'd asked her to marry him over thirty years ago. She pressed it into his bare palm. "Now do it right."

Dante glanced down at the ring, a flood of emotions rising up his throat. When he turned to Emma, he knew what he had to do.

Emma stared at the ring in his hand, her eyes wet with tears, her head shaking back and forth. "Don't. I don't need your pity."

"Pity? You think I'd get down on my knees in the snow because I pity you?" Dante slid off the gurney and dropped to one knee. "Emma Jennings, in the short time we've been together, we've been through a lot. You've saved my life more than once and you've shown me that I have so much more life to look forward to and I can't think of anyone I'd rather spend it with. Will you marry me?"

Emma's knees buckled and she dropped to the ground beside him. "Are you sure this is what you want?"

"I've never been more sure." He took her hand in his and removed her glove. "Marry me."

Tears slipped down her cheek even as snowflakes clung to her eyelashes and she nodded. He slipped the ring on her finger, feeling happiness bubble up inside him. He rose to his feet and lifted her up in his arms. "Mom, Pierce, Tuck, Maddox, meet my fiancée, the beautiful Emma Jennings. We're getting married."

"I thought you were already engaged," Pierce said.

Dante grinned and hugged Emma close. "Brother, in case you didn't know it already, it's all about the ring."

## Chapter Seventeen

Emma's pulse pounded and her hands shook as she stood in the hallway of the ranch house, wearing Amelia's beautiful wedding dress, awaiting her cue. When the strains of Mendelssohn's "Wedding March" blared over the sound system, she stepped forward.

Maddox, dressed in a black tuxedo, offered her his arm and walked her into the living room toward the big stone fireplace at the center, where Dante stood with his brothers on the left and his brothers' wives on the right, and the justice of the peace they'd brought in from Medora in the center.

Christmas morning was bright with sunshine and it promised to be the best day of Emma's life. Her heart was so full, she could barely breathe. It had all happened so fast. The entire Thunder Horse clan had pulled together to make the wedding happen in an incredibly short amount of time.

This was it. She was about to become Mrs. Thunder Horse.

Dante stood tall, his gunshot wound bandaged and hidden beneath the sleeve of his tuxedo. He'd combed his dark hair back and his green eyes flashed when she'd appeared.

Amelia sat in a front row chair with Sean sitting to

her right and what seemed like half of the Medora citizens seated in the other chairs filling the room. A huge Christmas tree stood in the corner, lights shining and a bright star crowning the top.

Through the window she could see fat white snowflakes falling and frost making pretty designs on the glass. The day couldn't have been more beautiful and the man she was about to marry more perfect.

Emma walked toward him wondering if this was all a dream and she'd wake up in her apartment cold and alone. But when Dante smiled, his green eyes shiny, she knew it was real.

He held out his hand and she took it, knowing he'd always be there for her.

"Emma Jennings, do you take Dante to be your husband? To love, honor and cherish so long as you both shall live?"

Emma spoke in clear voice, never more certain in her life of her answer, "I do."

"And, Dante, do you take Emma to be your wife—"

Dante lifted her hands and held them tight. "I do, to love honor and cherish so long as we both shall live. Can we wrap this up? I want to kiss my wife."

Laughter rose from the crowd as Dante did just that, kissing Emma in front of everyone. When he finally let her up for air, her cheeks were warm and she couldn't stop smiling.

The justice of the peace shrugged. "They said yes. Folks, meet Mr. and Mrs. Dante Thunder Horse. May the Great Spirit bless you both."

"You heard the man, the last Thunder Horse brother is hitched," Tuck said. "Our family is growing."

"Yeah, and it's about to get even bigger." Maddox slid an arm around Katya and grinned. "Katya's pregnant."

Tuck whooped. "I don't know how you found time, gallivanting all over the globe. And don't that just beat all?" He lifted his Lily in his arms and held her up. "Lily's going to be a sister. Julia and I are expecting our second."

"Uh—" Pierce raised a hand "—I was saving it until after the wedding, but Roxy and I are expecting, too."

Amelia clapped her hands to her mouth, her eyes alight. "All those grandbabies. I am truly blessed."

Everyone turned to Emma and Dante.

Tuck spoke. "Well? What are you two waiting for? Get busy so our kids can all grow up together."

"You heard them, Wife. Let's get crackin'." Dante swung Emma up in his arms and marched her out of the room.

Her heart swelled with the love she felt for this man and his entire family. Being married to a Thunder Horse was going to be everything she ever dreamed of and more. The Great Spirit had truly blessed them.

\* \* \* \* \*

# COMING NEXT MONTH FROM

# HARLEQUIN®

# INTRIGUE®

## Available October 21, 2014

### #1527 RUSTLING UP TROUBLE
*Sweetwater Ranch* • by Delores Fossen
Deputy Rayanne McKinnon believes ATF agent Blue McCurdy, father to her unborn child, is dead—until he shows up with hired killers on his trail and no memory of their night together.

### #1528 THE HUNK NEXT DOOR
*The Specialists* • by Debra Webb & Regan Black
Fearless Police Chief Abigail Jensen seized a drug shipment, halting the cash flow of an embedded terrorist cell. Can undercover specialist Riley O'Brien find the threat before the terrorists retaliate?

### #1529 BONEYARD RIDGE
*The Gates* • by Paula Graves
To save her from a deadly ambush, undercover P.I. Hunter Bragg takes Susannah Marsh on the run. But when their escape alerts a dangerous enemy from Susannah's past, Hunter will need to rely on the other members of The Gates to rescue the woman who healed his heart.

### #1530 CROSSFIRE CHRISTMAS
*The Precinct* • by Julie Miller
When injured undercover cop Charlie Nash kidnapped nurse Teresa Rodriguez to stitch up his wounds, he never meant to put his brave rescuer in danger...or fall in love with her.

### #1531 COLD CASE AT COBRA CREEK
by Rita Herron
Someone in town will do anything to stop Sage Freeport from getting the truth about her missing son. Tracker Dugan Graystone's offer to help is Sage's best chance to find her child...and lose her heart....

### #1532 NIGHT OF THE RAVEN
by Jenna Ryan
When an old curse is recreated by someone seeking revenge, only Ethan McVey, the mysterious new Raven's Cove police chief, stands between Amara Bellam and a brutal killer.

---

**YOU CAN FIND MORE INFORMATION ON UPCOMING HARLEQUIN® TITLES, FREE EXCERPTS AND MORE AT WWW.HARLEQUIN.COM.**

HICNM1014

# REQUEST YOUR FREE BOOKS!
## 2 FREE NOVELS PLUS 2 FREE GIFTS!

**H HARLEQUIN®**

# INTRIGUE®

## BREATHTAKING ROMANTIC SUSPENSE

**YES!** Please send me 2 FREE Harlequin Intrigue® novels and my 2 FREE gifts (gifts are worth about $10). After receiving them, if I don't wish to receive any more books, I can return the shipping statement marked "cancel." If I don't cancel, I will receive 6 brand-new novels every month and be billed just $4.74 per book in the U.S. or $5.24 per book in Canada. That's a savings of at least 14% off the cover price! It's quite a bargain! Shipping and handling is just 50¢ per book in the U.S. and 75¢ per book in Canada.* I understand that accepting the 2 free books and gifts places me under no obligation to buy anything. I can always return a shipment and cancel at any time. Even if I never buy another book, the two free books and gifts are mine to keep forever.

182/382 HDN F42N

| Name | (PLEASE PRINT) | |
|---|---|---|
| Address | | Apt. # |
| City | State/Prov. | Zip/Postal Code |

Signature (if under 18, a parent or guardian must sign)

Mail to the **Harlequin® Reader Service:**
**IN U.S.A.:** P.O. Box 1867, Buffalo, NY 14240-1867
**IN CANADA:** P.O. Box 609, Fort Erie, Ontario L2A 5X3

**Are you a subscriber to Harlequin Intrigue books
and want to receive the larger-print edition?
Call 1-800-873-8635 or visit www.ReaderService.com.**

* Terms and prices subject to change without notice. Prices do not include applicable taxes. Sales tax applicable in N.Y. Canadian residents will be charged applicable taxes. Offer not valid in Quebec. This offer is limited to one order per household. Not valid for current subscribers to Harlequin Intrigue books. All orders subject to credit approval. Credit or debit balances in a customer's account(s) may be offset by any other outstanding balance owed by or to the customer. Please allow 4 to 6 weeks for delivery. Offer available while quantities last.

**Your Privacy**—The Harlequin® Reader Service is committed to protecting your privacy. Our Privacy Policy is available online at www.ReaderService.com or upon request from the Harlequin Reader Service.

We make a portion of our mailing list available to reputable third parties that offer products we believe may interest you. If you prefer that we not exchange your name with third parties, or if you wish to clarify or modify your communication preferences, please visit us at www.ReaderService.com/consumerschoice or write to us at Harlequin Reader Service Preference Service, P.O. Box 9062, Buffalo, NY 14269. Include your complete name and address.

HI13R

SPECIAL EXCERPT FROM

**H** HARLEQUIN®

# I N T R I G U E

*A surprise attack on her family ranch reunites a pregnant
deputy with her baby's father—who supposedly died five
months ago...*

*Read on for an excerpt from*
*RUSTLING UP TROUBLE*
*by* USA TODAY *bestselling author*

## Delores Fossen

She put her hand on his back to steady him. Bare skin on
bare skin.

The hospital gown hardly qualified as a garment, with
one side completely off his bandaged shoulder. Judging
from the drafts he felt on various parts of his body, Rayanne
was probably getting an eyeful.

Of course, it apparently wasn't something she hadn't
already seen, since according to her they'd slept together
five months ago.

"Will saying I'm sorry help?" he mumbled, and because
he had no choice, he ditched the bargaining-position idea
and lay back down.

"Nothing will help. As soon as you're back on your feet,
I want you out of Sweetwater Springs and miles and miles
away from McKinnon land. Got that?"

Oh, yeah. It was crystal clear.

It didn't matter that he didn't know why he'd done the
things he had, but he'd screwed up. Maybe soon, Blue would
remember everything that he might be trying to forget.

HIEXP69794

Her phone rang, the sound shooting through the room. And his head. Rayanne fished the phone from her pocket, looked at the screen and then moved to the other side of the room to take the call. It occurred to him then that she might be involved with someone.

Five months was a long time.

And this someone might be calling to make sure she was okay.

Blue felt the twinge of jealousy that throbbed right along with the pain in various parts of his body, and he wished he could just wake up from this crazy nightmare that he was having.

"No, he doesn't remember," she said to whoever had called. She turned to look back at him, but her coat shifted to the side.

Just enough for Blue to see the stomach bulge beneath her clothes.

*Oh, man.*

It felt as if someone had sucked the air right out of his lungs. He didn't need his memory to understand what that meant.

Rayanne was pregnant.

*Find out how Rayanne reacts to Blue's discovery and what they plan to do to protect their unborn child when*
*RUSTLING UP TROUBLE*
*by USA TODAY bestselling author*
*Delores Fossen hits shelves in November 2014.*

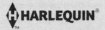

# INTRIGUE

## A NATIVE AMERICAN TRACKER MAKES IT HIS MISSION TO BRING HOME A MISSING CHILD JUST IN TIME FOR CHRISTMAS…

After two years, Sage Freeport had all but given up hope of seeing her little boy again…until she met Dugan Graystone. They shared a disdain for local law enforcement, the same folks who'd hindered Sage's efforts to find her son. As an expert tracker, the broad-shouldered Native American was sure he could find the child—even if he had to leave Texas to do it. Spending time with Sage, watching as she broke down every time a lead didn't pan out, Dugan worked harder than he ever had before. Now, with Christmas just days away, Dugan knew Sage trusted him to give her the greatest gift of all: bring Benji home….

# COLD CASE AT COBRA CREEK

## BY RITA HERRON

*Only from Harlequin® Intrigue®.*
*Available November 2014*
*wherever books and ebooks are sold.*

HI69798